DEVON LIBRARIES

Please return/renew this item by the due date.
Renew on tel. 0
www.devor

Hang the Hellion High

Bart Shannon, whose swift gun and air of competent assurance has carried him through several desperate encounters, is the sole survivor of a herding party bushwhacked by rustlers on the Arizona trail. He finds that a crooked sheriff in the pay of Zena Clayburne, a southern aristocrat, has sworn out a warrant, charging him with conspiracy in the rustling of the herd.

Hard and aggressive, Zena is determined to become the richest landowner in the state, and realizes that only Bart stands in her way. The smaller landowners are either murdered or forced to sell out on her terms, but Shannon has no intention of giving up his vow to hunt down the men who killed his companions and left him for dead.

On his own at first, he finally wins support and now there begins a vicious range war with no quarter given. Can Shannon win through?

Hang the Hellion High

Stephen Hartmann

A Black Horse Western

ROBERT HALE · LONDON

© John Glasby 1962, 2003
First hardcover edition 2003
Originally published in paperback as
Hang the Hellion High by Chuck Adams

ISBN 0 7090 7246 5

Robert Hale Limited
Clerkenwell House
Clerkenwell Green
London EC1R 0HT

The right of John Glasby to be
identified as author of this work has been
asserted by him in accordance with the Copyright,
Design and Patents Act 1988.

Typeset by
Derek Doyle & Associates, Liverpool.
Printed and bound in Great Britain by
Antony Rowe Limited, Wiltshire

CHAPTER I

TRAIL HERD

Three riders checked their mounts on a rise of ground which looked out over the vast, stretching valley leading over the Arizona trail. The sun was low on the western horizon, throwing long, huge shadows over the rocky ground, and they were all tired men who had ridden herd far and fast. The leader lifted his right hand, swaying a little in his saddle from weariness. His name was Bart Shannon, tall, broad-shouldered, with slender hips, the build of an athlete, clear grey eyes that took in everything in a single, sweeping glance, staring out over the land ahead from beneath thick, dark brows. The hands that held the reins lay loosely over the pommel of the saddle, long-fingered, fast when it came to drawing a gun.

The two men who sat their horses close behind him were both Texans – Brad Kenley and Jess Travis. Shannon ran a dry tongue over his lips, then turned his head tnd glanced back at the trail along which they had ridden, pushing forward ahead of the cattle. The herd was visible now, spread over ten square miles of country, a thronging mass of beef, moving quietly at the moment, milling forward over the rough, dry ground. Soon, however, if there had been rain within the past month, they would scent water and that would start them moving, heading for the river some fifteen miles up ahead, a

5

surging mass of muscle and meat which nothing would be able to stop.

'They're making up early,' said Travis suddenly. He lifted a long arm and pointed back along the trail.

'Be dark soon,' muttered Bart harshly. 'No point in pushing them much further before night. If they get wind of the water, nothing will hold 'em.' He eyed the herd for a moment, then glanced off slightly to where the sun was setting in a mass of gathering yellow cloud. 'Could be a storm brewing out there by the look of the sky. There may be rain tonight.'

'Can't figger why Dodson picked this trail to bring the herd,' muttered Kenley shortly. He sucked in his grizzled cheeks. 'Means more than a hundred extra miles to ride and takes up through the worst territory in the State. Why didn't he use the northern trail if he wanted to git his beef to the market at Abilene in time for the best prices?'

Bart studied the sky for a further minute before answering. 'Chances are that he wants to get as many head as he can. This is a punishing trail for cattle, but at least we're off the beaten trail as far as bushwhackers and rustlers are concerned.' His eyes were cold as his glance swept over the two men. 'Dodson's no fool. He's heard the talk as far back as Kansas City, just the same as we have. There's a well-organized band working in this territory, and he ain't taking no chances on losing the best part of his herd.'

'You figger we'll miss them if we keep to this trail?' asked Kenley.

'Perhaps. If they do find the herd, they'll fight to get it. Once we're over the river and into Arizona, I'll feel safer.' He pulled hard on the reins, wheeled the horse and rode back down the rise. The herd were being bedded down for the night by the time they reached the camp. It was almost dark now, and the stars stood out like beacons in the clear sky overhead, but down in the west the thick storm clouds continued to gather, swarming out of the horizon where the sun had gone down, threatening to cover the whole of the sky. A wind had risen, kicking up the dust eddies from the dry ground. The herd was restless. Bart threw them a swiftly apprehensive glance as he slid from the saddle and watered his mount.

Dodson rode into the camp a while later, a bull-necked brute of a man, tall and broad, with skin that had been weathered to the colour and texture of old leather. The hands which held the reins were like his body with thick, hairy wrists; the fingers short and blunt, square-tipped, the heavy guns low at his waist. Bart's eyes watched him quietly from beneath the dark brows. Perhaps the other was thinking of the ride which still lay ahead of them, through the Bad Country just beyond the river, or maybe of closer things, the storm which was blowing up, wondering how the herd would react to it, always thinking of the possibility of stampede. Perhaps he was thinking of other things entirely. For Dodson's thoughts were always hidden things, even from the men who worked with him, who rode the same trail.

The storm began an hour before midnight. At first, there was only the faint flickering of the lightning as it raced across the western horizon in grey flashes of light accompanied by the dull, equally faint rumble of thunder, a low, ominous sound. Then it swept closer. The herd moved restlessly, a sea of horns and surging shapes. In the camp, the men waited and threw anxious eyes in the direction of the incoming clouds.

Bart drew the leather lashings of his jacket more tightly together as the cold night air crept in around his body. Dodson kept the riders on the move now that the storm was ready to strike in its full fury. The outriders rode the perimeter of the huge herd, keeping the frightened steers together, knowing that once they began to panic, nothing could possibly hold them until they reached the natural barrier of the distant river.

Bart threw uneasy eyes at the storm clouds. Perhaps it would have been best if Dodson had given the word to set the

7

cattle moving towards the river. They would have to head for it on the morrow and it would mean that the steers would have a trail to follow and it might lessen the possibility of a full-scale stampede. With lightning flashing in the near distance, it needed very little to start these critters panicking and he doubted it they could hold them once they were on the move. The dark curtain of the rain swept in with a startling suddenness and was upon them almost before they realized it. To the old riders, this storm was nothing new, but nevertheless, it was still a very frightening thing, not so much because of the storm itself, but for what they knew it could do to a herd of several thousand head of cattle. Bart raced his stud along the outer perimeter of the herd, the cavernous bellowing sounding in his ears as he urged the rest of the men to prod the weary, restless cattle back whenever they threatened to move out. The leaders had to be thrown off the trail, no matter what happened. Once they began to lead the way, everything would be finished and there would be nothing for it but to let them race for the river and try to halt them there before they plunged across, into a river possibly swollen by flood water, and hit the far bank. Lightning forked over the heavens now, the thunder booming directly overhead. It rang in his ears as he urged the weary stud forward, kicking with his spurs whenever the animal showed signs of faltering. Sleep leaded his own eyelids, but he forced them to remain open. There was danger here, a fresh danger which made its appearance a little while later. Even though he had been on the look-out for it, he almost missed it when it began. The solid blanket of rain had struck the herd a few moments earlier. Now it eased slightly and screwing his eyes against the darkness, he saw an eerie purple glow that flicked from the horns of the steers. An electrical display that danced from one beast to the next. Thudding forward, unnerved and howling in fright, the beasts thundered forward as the riders strove desperately to keep them milling. The men needed no orders now from anyone. Every man knew what to do, what was expected of him. Each blue-white fork of lightning which lit the heavens in a single violent sheet of flame, showed the herd on the point of stampeding.

'Keep them milling.' Although Dodson, riding shoulder with Bart yelled the words furiously at the top of his voice, the wind and rain snatched them from his lips and they were but a faint echo of themselves when Bart heard them. But the gesture that the other made was unmistakable and no words were needed. Smoothly, he pulled the gun from its holster, fired it three times into the air as the stud raced alongside the herd. They began to turn. Slowly at first, then more swiftly as a ripple spread along the solid front of cattle. For a moment it seemed that they would succeed even in the face of the storm fury that had closed about them. The herd held for what seemed an eternity. Then all hell was let loose as a lightning bolt struck home. Bart felt his mount rear in terror. He flung up his hand in front of his face in reflex instinct, eyes slitted against the glare. Rain beat heavily against his face, dripping from the brim of his hat. A moment later, and it was too late to do anything. The herd was on the move.

'Ride them out to the river,' yelled Dodson. He reined his mount as the massive herd thundered past. Bart nodded to show that he understood. Once a herd of this size – close on fifteen thousand head, started on a stampeded run, driven by the full fury of an Arizona storm, the only thing to do was to let them have their head and live in the hope that it might be possible to head them off in the right direction where they could do no damage and could be rounded up with the least trouble once they had run themselves down.

He kicked his horse, felt it respond wearily but gallantly. Whatever happened they didn't want this herd spread too far and wide. Those outlaws and rustlers might not always choose the northern trail and even now they might have got around to realizing that there were rich prizes slipping past them, through their fingers, further to the south.

Rain beat at him with a fury that was unlike anything he

had ever known before. It ran in rivulets down his face, into his eyes, soaking into his clothing until it hung limply against his body. The night was a savage, primeval thing as they rode after the herd. At first, the steers moved blindly, a racing river of solid muscle and thundering hoofs. But soon, riding both flanks, the men had them running in the right direction, over the level ground, towards the distant river. This was the business of driving herd. This was why they had been brought along, something for tired, bone-weary men to take in their stride.

Slowly, the storm died. The thunder and the flashing forks of lightning moved to the east and the rain slackened until it finally died away altogether. The herd surged forward, a few stragglers falling back, but the mass still keeping up with the leaders. Overhead and to the west, the sky was clear now. The stars shone brilliantly, so close that he felt he had only to reach up in the saddle to touch them with his outstretched fingers. Behind him, the storm had moved down close to the eastern horizon, was hugging the skyline, with an occasional distant flash of lightning. Bart lifted his head and peered into the night which stretched away in front of him, eyes narrowed a little. A flash of lightning, a rumble of thunder behind him, and he saw the herd as a line of dark shadow on the skyline. He gigged his mount and rode swiftly towards it.

Daybreak found them on the eastern bank of the wide river where it foamed over a stony bed. Further upstream it was in flood – a full flood brought on by the torrential rain of the previous night. The milling herd, quieted now that the storm had passed, were still on the eastern side, ready for the crossing. In the camp, half a dozen fires were lit and the men, wet and bone-weary, sat around them while the sun rose and the moisture streamed from their clothing. Bart Shannon shifted his body into a more comfortable position. His chest was warmed by the heat of the fire, but the cold air of dawn was still on his back and he shivered a little. Dodson strode in from riding the perimeter of the herd. He squatted next to the fire, took the plate of beans and jerky beef that Bart handed him and sat back. He chewed reflectively for a while, then studied Bart from beneath lowered brows.

'We lost a few head in that storm,' he said harshly. 'Reckon there must be a couple of hundred back there in the gullies. No point in riding back for 'em now. We've got to get these across this river today.'

'You figure we may run into trouble?' It was more of a statement than a question, but the other nodded slowly, scooped his plate clean.

'Could be. This is bad country to drive herd through.' He jerked an arm in the direction of the far bank of the river. For part of the way, two hundred yards maybe, the ground was soft and marshy and beyond, it opened out into a rocky gorge, dotted here and there with clumps of stunted trees and thorn. They would obviously have to ride for several miles before they came out into open prairie again.

'How about trying to ford the river further upstream – or even downstream?'

'Not a chance. I've had a couple of men scouting along the bank. Runs into a deep gorge three miles upstream. The other way, it's so swollen that we'd lose a thousand head or more trying to get them across. This is the only place where we stand any chance at all.'

'So we cross here and take whatever comes on the other side.' Bart nodded. For once he could guess at the other's thoughts. Dodson was not afraid of the rough country over the river, but of the rustlers and outlaws who could be hiding there. There were fourteen men in the camp; all of them handy with a gun and ready to fight if they had to, in order to get the herd through to Abilene. But there were times when even fourteen men such as his were not enough. Dodson was staking a lot in bringing the herd this way, along the southern trail.

The sun came up over the distant rim of the world, laid a red light over everything. Half an hour later, the sun higher

11

in the heavens, they began the crossing. The leaders went into the river, began to swim as the men rode alongside them, prodding them forward, urging them on with loud cries. It was hard work, dangerous work. The river was deep even here, swollen by the heavy rains, and there was a strong current flowing, swirling about the animals as they began to swim, following the current for a little way as they struck out for the further shore. Denver and Hale, men from the east, rode their mounts easily in midstream, easing the long horned animals in a wide U over the swiftly flowing water. The first of the cattle reached the other side, pulled themselves out of the clinging current on sliding hoofs and stood bellowing fiercely on the high, marshy ground, before moving forward a little way on to drier ground.

Sitting high in the saddle, Bart threw a thankful glance in their direction. Once a handful of the steers made it across, the others would follow almost automatically. This had been the worst and most difficult part of the crossing. Denver swung his horse about as part of the herd threatened to cut loose from the main bunch. He crowded close to the herd, dangerously close to the lowering, tossing horns, keeping them in motion. A good man who knew just how close he could go without exposing himself to any real danger.

But even an experienced cowman like that could make one mistake. It happened with the speed and suddenness of lightning. Had he not been keeping his eyes on the man, there would have been no chance at all of saving him. Denver's mount was almost in the shallows on the far bank when the steer broke loose with a bellowing roar. The horns, lowered, struck the mount in the chest, just beneath the breastbone. It reared savagely, instinctively, thrashing with two flailing forelegs as the pointed tip of the horn pulled away flesh and bone.

Denver was thrown from the saddle, pitching backward into the muddy water as his mount fell sideways from under him. Without pausing to think, Bart kicked his own stud

12

forward, feeling it surge through the water powerfully as the spurs raked its sides. An instant and Denver was in the water, on his feet, maintaining his balance with difficulty against the swirling water that sucked hungrily about his waist, safe for a split second but with death only a few feet away as the herd moved in on him. He lifted his right hand as Bart rode in on him. The nearest steer was less than three feet away when Bart caught hold of the other's wrist, pulling hard on it, dragging Denver through water and mud, away from the beasts, towards the bank.

'Get behind those rocks and stay there,' cried Bart loudly. He pointed and released the other's wrist. Denver nodded quickly to indicate that he understood. Before he had time to move, Bart was back in the river, urging his stud towards the herd. Here, with the badly injured horse still floundering helplessly in mid-stream, they threatened to break, to come surging in a solid wall, away from the others. It was over an hour before the herd was safely over, strung out over three miles of the rough, coarse ground over the river. Bart slid from the saddle and threw a quick, appraising glance over there, then turned to face Dodson.

The big man rubbed a hand over his stubbled chin. 'Better than I thought when I saw them start across,' he said roughly. 'We haven't lost many on the trail this far. But there's more dangerous country up ahead, I can sense it. Coyotes and wolves and men who probably have the habits of both.'

'You think they may have moved as far south as this?' Bart lifted his brows into an interrogatory line. He looked out over the endless plains that reached out to the far horizons.

Something flared at the back of the other's eyes, something deep and incredibly remote. Finally, he said quietly, 'If they have, this is the most likely place they'll try to attack the herd. Plenty of cover, the river at our backs and the cattle safely over. Yes, if they intend to make a try for the herd, we can expect trouble soon.'

'I'll warn the rest of the men.' Bart rose to his full height, turned towards the horse beside him. But even as he moved, a shot hammered out against the stillness, a sharp explosive sound that jerked up his head, turning it swiftly in the direction from which the shot had come. The cattle were nearly all well clear of the river now, milling aimlessly in the rough rock half a mile away. But there was one of the men, his horse still in the marsh ground; a man who, even as Bart watched, slid slowly from his saddle and pitched forward into the soft, green earth, to lie still, while his horse plunged forward. Fanning out around the rising curve of the rocks, came the riders, racing past the herd, firing as they came. There were others crouched down among the shadowed gullies with rifles and whining lead hummed across the plain as Bart went down on one knee beside the kicking horse, the guns sliding from their holsters with faintly heard whispers of sound. They kicked against his wrists as he brought them to bear on the approaching men. He knew that there was real danger from the men who were trying to ride them down, trying to scatter the herd and start a stampede, away from the river. But with the cold-edged calculation and knowledge which had been born in him over the years of riding the trails of the frontier country, he was already watching the trail further to the south-west, scanning the steep walls of the tall, rearing, redstone canyons. Almost two hundred yards from the edge of the marsh where the first man had fallen, he could make out the stabbing lances of light, just visible in the sunlight, the muzzle flashes of high-powered Winchesters. The outlaws had planned their attack well, had obviously followed their trail from far back to the east and had lain in wait for them through the night, possibly knowing that the violence of the storm would drive the steers to the river in double-quick time. He moistened his lips, fired twice and saw two of the men roll out of their saddles and pitch forward to the ground with bullets in their chests.

'They're stampeding the herd,' yelled Travis wildly. He lifted his head to point in the direction of the small bunch of men, expertly working the steers forward, driving them towards the high wall with wild shouts and shots from their guns.

'Forget the herd,' shouted Bart hoarsely. 'Get those riders out there. Shoot them down.' It was the only chance they had. The men crouched among the rocks were now able to shoot down upon them and there was little cover here along the bank of the river. He pushed himself to his feet, fired a handful of shots at a bunch of yelling riders and scuttled for cover as lead kicked up gouts of dirt and water about his body. Dodson was close behind him, running forward, his head low on the bull neck. His eyes were glazed slightly, face twisted into a grimace of frustrated anger. It was grim business. Grim and cold. Shooting down men whenever they came within range of their guns, reloading the empty chambers while crouched behind one of the low, stunted bushes, knowing that all the time one was an almost perfect target for the riflemen in the rocks. If only they could finish off a few of them they might stand a good chance, thought Bart fiercely. He threw a swiftly apprehensive glance in the direction of the red sandstone bluffs. They shone eerily in the strengthening sunlight, and by slitting his eyes against the glare, he could just make out the dark shape of a man who exposed himself for a second as he took aim at the men below him. He snapped a sudden shot at the shadow as it ducked back under cover, but from that distance, it was impossible to tell whether his shot had found its mark.

Gun thunder echoed back from the rising escarpments as the men settled down to kill or be killed. Deep down inside, Bart knew the score as far as these rustling outlaws were concerned. They had heard some of the stories as far back as Broken Wheel, the last small township through which they had passed before hitting the Badlands of the State frontier. These men were said to be operating on behalf of one of the big ranchers further to the north, rustling the cattle, changing the brands until they could be safely absorbed into the

15

main herd; a crooked rancher who seemed to know of every herd that passed through this territory.

Whoever these outlaws were they knew every trick of this kind of fighting. Splitting their groups, taking care not to get into the direct line of fire of the rest of the party in the rocks, they circled the men hemmed in on the bank of the river, firing incessantly, riding their horses in a curious zig-zag fashion, obviously learned from the Indians, making them doubly difficult to hit.

There was now an icy coldness in Bart's brain, washing away everything else. Guns against guns with the men reloading quickly now, pouring bullets into the outlaws. A death-laden slug whined through the brush close to Bart's head. He turned quickly, looked across at Dodson where the trail master lay in the marsh, aiming and firing swiftly, with each bullet taking its toll of the men who tried to crowd them down. Bart felt a little shiver pass through him as he watched the huge, bull-necked man working at this trade of death; a man who smiled almost continually as he killed as though he were enjoying the thing that he was doing, a calm dispassionate expression on his face.

Bart counted his hits slowly, doing his best to kill the men in the rocks, the direction from which the greatest danger came. They were in a position to kill and yet sufficiently out of range to make it difficult to drop them with Colts. Yet four of them had died, their bodies pitching down the sheer side of the redstone bluffs. How many more there were, still hidden up there, training their Winchesters on the men below, it was impossible to tell.

It was equally impossible to estimate how many of the herders were still alive. He could see seven of them stretched out on the ground almost directly in front of him, and as none of them moved, he guessed they were either dead or seriously wounded. The ranks of the outlaws had been thinned drastically too by their accurate and direct fire. More shots from the rifles hummed over his head like a cloud of hornets and he ducked low in reflex movement, pulling his head down into the brown, stinking mud, feeling it clog his mouth and nostrils so that he could scarcely breathe. The shooting died a little and he pulled his face clear of the muck, staring about him through eyes that were now a flint grey, narrowed with sudden purpose. Beside him, Dodson eased himself back on to his haunches with a pain-filled expression on his bluff features. He nursed a shoulder that showed blood between his clenched fingers where a bullet had torn through muscle and flesh.

He waved Bart back as the other made to crawl forward. 'Forget about the shoulder,' he hissed sharply. 'Only a flesh wound. Won't stop me none when they come in again – and they will come again, now they know that there are some of us still alive and kicking. Because if they don't, we'll go right on after them until we catch up with them and when we do, I want you and the others who are still with me, to help me string them up from the nearest tree. They've stolen the herd, bushwhacked it.'

Bart threw a quick glance along the trail leading up from the river, stretching away to the south and west. There was a faint cloud of dust now visible in the sunlight and at the back of it, he thought he could just make out a solid mass of colour where the herd was still racing away, being stampeded and driven by the outlaws. Then, for a moment, he forgot the herd, forgot the long drive which lay behind them. The outlaws, mounted on fleet sorrels, were moving in again, this time for the kill.

Down and up, Bart lifted the long-barrelled guns in a sweeping draw which lined them up on the first of the two riders as they swept in to the attack. The hammers slammed on the cartridges and the guns kicked against his wrists almost before the sights had come to bear. He fired as if by instinct, but there was nothing careless about the bullets which took the two leading riders clean through their heads and knocked them backwards out of their saddles, the rider-

17

less horses plunging on. Beside Bart, Dodson moved more slowly. Pain and the loss of blood that pulsed from the deep wound in his shoulder had slowed up the fast draw, had shaken his aim slightly, His face was beaded with sweat and it was beginning to run down into the half-closed eyes as they slitted themselves painfully against the harsh glare of the sun, the muscles of his huge arms standing out under the tight cloth of the fringed jacket as he forced himself to bring the heavy guns to bear on these yelling men who had taken away the herd from him. Pressure was taken on the triggers, but it was impossible for him to pull one of them, the one held by the hand that trailed blood into the marshy ground. His teeth showed through the lips which were curled back in a tight, angry grin and the veins throbbed in the thick, bull-like neck, twisting and straining as he fought to keep a tight hold on his consciousness and take some of these killers with him if he had to die. Scarlet veins leapt and pulsed and still he could fire only one of the guns. His first shot, pulled by the weakness in his body, went wild, missed the riding man who crowded close, firing from the saddle as he bored in. More sound hammered against the silence as he fired again. This time his bullet found its mark, took the man in the right shoulder, spinning him round in the saddle as if he had been slammed by a heavy, tight-fisted blow.

He held on to the pommel grimly as the horse swept him past, less than ten yards away. Slowly, as if the muscles were reluctant to fight against the strain, Dodson lowered his arm, his shoulders slumping forward into the mud. The eyes, Bart noticed, with a feeling of surprise, were glazing over swiftly. With a sudden curse, he moved sideways until he had reached Dodson, rolled him over swiftly, fingers probing for the wound, pulling the bloodsoaked shirt to one side.

Weakly, Dodson shook his head, his eyes striving to hold some of the life in them as his lips moved. 'No use,' he gasped, forcing the words out. 'No use at all. Thought I'd get out of this alive and even the score with these killers, but I ain't going to make it.' He swallowed, head slumping forward a little. For a moment, Bart felt sure he was gone, and he lifted his head to stare after the riders who were pulling their horses around swiftly in a widening circle as they headed hack towards the redstone bluffs. Then, fighting for every breath, the other went on hoarsely; 'I've been watching you, Bart, while you've been riding herd for me. You can git out of this mess alive if you've a mind to. And you're fast with a gun, mighty fast. Get these skunks who've done this, ride 'em down clear across the territory if you have to, but kill them.' There was an edge of hatred to his voice, of harsh anger at what had happened, a hatred and anger that gave strength back for a moment into the spent body, 'Find who's at the back of this, finish it for me, Bart.'

'I'll do that,' the other promised. There was no tremor in his voice now, only a deep and calm quiet which made it sound even more ominous than the other's. For a fraction of a second, there seemed to be a gleam of satisfaction flitting over the other's face, then he gave a deep sigh and slipped to the ground, his huge, hairy arms stretched out in the soft, moisture-laden earth, the guns in his fingers falling into the dirt as they loosened their grip.

For what seemed an eternity, the other knelt beside Dodson's body, then he looked down at the guns in his hands as though seeing them properly for the first time. His fingers were quite steady as he plucked the cartridges from his belt and thrust them into the empty chambers. Finally, he was satisfied. Getting to his feet, he moved forward, in the direction of the sandstone bluffs. There was now no sign of the men on horseback, but he guessed that they had not withdrawn very far and would return very soon to make certain that they had killed every man in the herding party. They could not afford to leave a single man alive, a man who could testify against them if he got out of this god-forsaken place alive.

He found a narrow trail in the base of the bluffs, a trail

that led upwards to where he had seen the men hidden, men with rifles who had killed as many of his companions as those on horseback. He began to climb with a silent anger that burned deep within him, washing all weariness from his brain, filling him with a terrible singleness of purpose that transcended anything he had ever experienced before. There was a stand of brush at the bend in the trail and he went forward cautiously now. The men up here may have pulled back once they had seen that their part in the attack was finished. This was a good place, it commanded an excellent view of the river below. He ran his tongue over his lips, feeling it stick to the dryness that was on them.

He could hear nothing. Then, down below, there was the sound of hoofs drumming on the hard ground. A few scattered shots, the echoes chasing themselves up into the bluffs. Then silence. He knew now, with a sick certainty, that none of the other men who had ridden herd with him, were still alive. The outlaws had done their work well. But he still had the memories of their faces burned deeply into his brain, pictures that he knew he would carry with him until he died. And he was still alive. He gritted his teeth and began to edge his way forward, over the rocks.

Now he was less than twenty feet from the brush. Narrowing his eyes, he paused and watched it closely, shifting his eyes then from side to side a little, never keeping them still. Nothing moved there. It made sense that the men here would slip away once they had killed most of the men below. There was nothing for them to wait for, no chance that anyone would be foolish enough to try to make a break for the bluffs and start to climb, a man with a terrible vengeance in his heart, burning at his vitals . . .

He reached the brush, edged around it, eyes alert. The trail widened a little here and he caught a glimpse of hoof marks in the loose soil. So they had brought their horses up here too, he reflected. Funny that he had not heard them riding away. He pulled himself back behind the cover of the brush as the sudden realization struck him that this could he a trap, that they might have anticipated such a move on his part.

Quick as he was, his movements were too slow. The crash of the shot came in an angry surge of sound which bellowed at him from the rising, rocky walls, red in the streaming sunlight. He gasped and swayed backward, clutching desperately at the out-thrusting branches of the brush as the red-hot slug took him in the shoulder. His right arm went dead, the gun slipping from his nerveless fingers, clattering down among the rocks.

There came a sudden harsh laugh from somewhere directly ahead of him as he tried to bring the long barrel of his other gun to bear on the sound. A shadow stepped forward into view and came towards him. Through pain-blurred eyes he fought to make out the details of the man who strode along the trail, feet scuffing up the dry dust; a bearded giant of a man with a wide, leering mouth and broken, stained teeth that showed in a snarl of savage delight.

'I'm going to kill you, stranger.' It was quite simply said, but every word which the other uttered carried with it the certainty of death, not a threat but a promise. Another step and it was difficult to see the man as his features blurred and swayed behind a red curtain of pain. Bart drew in a deep, rasping breath, tried to clear his vision, tried with a desperate anger to lift the gun in his left hand, to bring the barrel to bear on the other's chest, knowing that the killer's gun was almost lined up on his chest, that the thick finger was beginning to tighten on the trigger. He could feel the stain on the front of his shirt begin to trickle wetly down his chest, towards the heavy belt at his waist. There was blood beginning to gather on the dry, dusty trail beneath him.

'We can't have witnesses whenever we take a herd like this.' A wide, leering grin, the circular black hole at the end of the gun barrel, a finger that gleamed whitely as it tightened relentlessly.

Sweat beaded Bart's forehead in that split second and began to twist in tiny streams down his cheeks and on to his lean jaw. Somehow, in spite of the weakness in his body, he managed to squeeze the trigger of his gun. It kicked wildly, but the bullet found its mark in the killer's leg. For a moment, he stood swaying as his leg threatened to give under his weight, then he moved back and stood with his shoulders against the smooth rock behind him and the grin on his lips merely widened still further. Death was an inch and a split second away as Bart threw himself savagely, instinctively, to one side, thrusting backward with his powerful legs. The bullet smashed into the boulder beside him, where his head had been a moment earlier. But unlike the killer, there was no solid rock at his back, only a foot of trail and then emptiness.

He felt the ground give way under him, threw out his injured arm in an effort to keep his balance, but failed. His fingertips brushed the rough edge of the up-thrusting rock as he fell over the rim of the trail, pitching down into the emptiness. Only vaguely was he aware of the redstone walls flashing past his body at a dizzying speed. Then he hit something hard and solid and there was darkness in his brain . . .

As he fought his way slowly back to consciousness, Bart could feel the coldness on his face and when he finally forced his eyes to open, and stay open, there was nothing in front of them that he could see, only a deep and remote darkness which made him think for one long moment, that he was still unconscious, or blind. With an effort, he tried to move his legs. Pain jarred redly through his body with every tiny movement he made but he gritted his teeth and kept on trying, knowing that he had to move if he was to stay alive. Five pain-filled minutes later, he sat with his back and shoulders against the rough rock and drew a deep breath into his lungs. Fire still seemed to burn in his shoulder and chest where the heavy slug still lay somewhere in his flesh, buried close to the bone. It was night and there was a cold, yellow-white moon lying low on the eastern horizon, and the stars stood out hard and diamond-brilliant over his head. As his eyes grew accustomed to the darkness, he saw what he had begun to suspect, that he was not at the bottom of the bluffs, but only a part of the way down, where a thorn bush had somehow broken his fall and allowed his unconscious body to slip a couple of feet to a wide, rock-strewn ledge. Now he sat with his back to the canyon face and his legs thrust out straight in front of him, towards the empty edge of the ledge. How far down it was to the ground below, he could not guess, but he was certain of one thing; that if he had fallen the whole of the way and that bush had not broken his fall, he would not have been alive at that moment.

In the thirty minutes that followed, he tried to patch up his shoulder as best he could with strips of cloth torn from his shirt. Then he examined the rest of his body for broken bones. His left ankle was swollen to almost twice its normal size and it was agony to put his weight on it. His body seemed to have been crushed and bruised all over and every movement he made was pure agony. But somehow, he told himself fiercely, he had to get down off this bluff and try to find one of the horses that might still be roaming around close to the massacre. On foot, he stood no chance at all of getting out of this place alive. On horseback, the chances were almost as remote, but there was water here for him to take with him, and it was just possible that he could follow the trail left by the others. He doubted if they would be taking any special precautions to hide their trail north, believing as they did that every man had been killed. And besides, he reflected, as reason re-asserted itself, it would not be easy to hide the trail left by several thousand head of beef cattle on the run.

The next three hours were things torn from a nightmare. Only by sheer iron will and the memory of the promise he had made to Dodson before he had died, made it possible for him to make his way down the side of the bluff, moving in almost complete darkness, a few steps at a time, pausing often for breath and to allow some of the strength to come back into his battered muscles and limbs. He had a job to do, he kept reminding himself. He had to track down these killers, find out who lay at the back of them, and see that his companions were avenged.

When he reached the flat, marshy ground, it was almost dawn. The stars were starting to dim in the east and there was a pale grey flush spreading up from just below the distant horizon. The air still held a chill touch, but very soon, once the sun came up, it would be as hot as the hinges of hell. He washed the wound in his shoulder at the river and splashed the cold, muddy water on to his fact and hair, shocking some of the life back into his body. Finally, he bound a strip of cloth as tightly as he could around his injured ankle, certain now that no bones were broken, but that it would not carry him for long without support.

On one of the dead outlaws, he found two guns, took all of the slugs he could find, then filled his canteen and began to move through the soft, clinging soil towards the rocks in the distance. It was unlikely that the horses, still alive, would have gone very far, unless the outlaws had rounded them all up and taken the animals with them when they had ridden off some time during the night. If they had, then he was finished. He could not hope to cross fifty miles of desert country on foot in his present condition.

CHAPTER II

GUNFIGHTER

High noon saw a solitary horseman riding north-west across the terrible, sun-baked desert country which bordered the southern trail. A man who leaned forward heavily in the saddle, eyes glazed, the wide-brimmed hat falling over his eyes and staying there as if he lacked even the strength to lift his head and jerk it back into place. Bart Shannon had run the mount to earth less than an hour after the grey dawn had brightened in the east, recognizing it as the horse which had belonged to Dodson himself. Evidently, the outlaws had taken every mount they could round up, but had overlooked this particular horse among the rocks where it had wandered during the height of the gun battle. It had not been an easy thing to hem it in against the solid wall of rock and then throw the lariat which had finally settled over the frightened animal's neck and he had almost reached the end of his endurance before he had succeeded in mounting and hanging on like grim death while the horse bucked and kicked for several moments, before settling down.

Now, they were riding slowly across the blazing face of the Badlands, following a trail which was almost obliterated in places where the shifting alkali had been blown over it by the wind which had risen and now blew steadily from the south-west, carrying the hot grains of sand on its breath, sand which worked its way irritatingly into the folds of his skin and down the back of his burning throat. The sips from the canteen were becoming more and more frequent now, doing little to ease the raging thirst and cool his hot mouth and throat. He knew that he had to conserve his water if he was to have any chance of survival but with the dust devils dancing and whirling at the edge of his vision and the red haze dancing continually in front of his eyes as the rays of the blistering sun beat down upon his neck and shoulders, it was becoming more and more impossible to force himself to go on without drinking from his precious, and dwindling water supply.

The outlaws had set a punishing pace for the herd, driving it far more quickly than they should. Probably they were afraid, knowing they had more miles to cover now that they had been forced to watch this little-used trail to the south. Not until those brand marks had been changed would they really feel safe. He tried to shift himself into a more comfortable position in the saddle, but every move he made threatened to open the slug wound in his shoulder and there was the faintness in his body which came from loss of blood. Only the iron determination kept him going through that terrible, gruelling day; a day of heat and thirst, pain and weariness in which a horse plodded forward slowly and a grim savage man held on tightly, knowing with a sick certainty that once he fell from the saddle to the ground, he would never find the strength necessary to remount.

There was no respite from the sun for the whole of that day and when night came, sweeping in from the east on the heels of the flaming red line of light that marked the place where the sun had gone down, the transition from heat to cold was as sudden as the setting of the sun itself. The sky was clear. No clouds there tonight to hold in the heat. Bart shivered, drew his jacket more tightly about his shoulders, sucked in deep breaths of the raw night air and fought savagely to keep his head clear. There had been long moments during the afternoon, when he had found his mind wandering, when the thoughts that went through his brain had made no sense on looking back at them; and he doubted if he could face another day such as that and remain sane.

The horse was moving slowly now. It had not drunk since they had left the river more than twelve hours earlier and the tremendous heat of the day had not helped its stamina any. How much longer before he reached the edge of this desert country, he wondered dully? Perhaps he was moving around in a big circle and he would find himself back at the river at sun-up. The thought almost broke him in half and he pushed it out of his mind instantly, refusing to think about that possibility. In the darkness, it was almost impossible to follow the trail left by the herd. Unwounded and fresh, he would have spotted it with ease even in the blackest hour of the night. But now it was difficult to keep his eyes focused on the ground in front of him.

An hour passed. Then another and still the air seemed to grow colder. The tough little range horse somehow forced itself to move and after what seemed an eternity, the country changed, the desert wastes gave way to brush and then, shortly before dawn, to strands of tall, black willow which bordered on more pleasant country. At times, Bart stopped his mount and bent forward over the pommel as far as possible, the fingers of his left hand tightening on the reins to prevent himself from losing his balance. Always, after a few moments of searching, he managed to find evidence that cattle had been driven through there and he kicked the spur on his uninjured foot against the horse's flank, prodding it forward again.

When dawn did brighten, he found himself on a low rise, overlooking a broad valley. In the distance, he could just make out the cluster of buildings of a small township, lying near the far rim of the valley. The trail left by the herd forked here and he sat, swaying in the saddle, for a long moment, debating which to follow. His fuddled brain refused to function properly now and the bitter cold which had eaten its way deep into his vitals, had stiffened his muscles and limbs. The gaping hole in his shoulder had stopped bleeding now and it felt so numb that there was little pain. But he knew that he had to get help as quickly as possible if he was to stay alive and carry out his promise to Dodson.

He gigged the horse down the slope, a horse that was almost spent after the long, hard ride through the night and the heat of the previous day. There was a deadly calm in the valley as he made his way forward, a slowly climbing tenseness which could be felt rather than sensed. There was no sign of the herd. They had passed through here several hours before and in his present condition he knew that he stood no chance of following them.

There was a small ranch less than half a mile away, off the beaten trail, a low-roofed house which nestled in a small, irregularly-shaped valley at the bottom of a gently sloping bowl in the low hills, protected here from any of the winds which would whistle over this land in the winter. It looked, even from that distance, to be a place of lush and verdant crops and one could easily tell that there was no lack of irrigation here. A small herd grazed peacefully on one of the green slopes beyond the homestead and in the middle of the yard, he noticed that water gushed incessantly from the artesian zanja, flowing freely along the little troughs over all of the tilled land near the house. Flanking the homestead like a curved hand was the southern slope of a high ridge, filled with a substantial stand of good timber which would serve to break the winter storms.

Bart touched his lips with the tip of his tongue. Unconsciousness was not very far away now, he knew instinctively and he fought to hold on grimly as he felt his fingers begin to loosen on the reins. The iron will and determination which had carried him across more than fifty miles of inhospitable desert was ready to slip away from him now that he had finally made it. Still he hung in the saddle as his horse plodded wearily forward, into the small courtyard, its hoofs ringing on the hard ground. For a long moment, there was no sign from the house that his presence had been noticed. Then, without warning, there was a sudden spurt of flame from one of the windows, a spurt that he saw a split second before the sharp, angry report of the rifle reached his ears. He jerked back in the saddle as he felt the wind of the bullet fanning his cheek.

He reined in close a moment later, knowing that there might be no second warning, that whoever had fired that shot had intended to miss him. There was a cover porch which spanned the whole length of the ranch and with an effort he tried to peer through the curtain covered windows to make out the identity of the person who had fired on him, ready to call out whenever he saw them. It was as he started to swing down from the saddle, holding on with his good hand, that the door was opened abruptly and the long barrel of a Winchester was thrust out in his direction. A woman's clear and resonant voice called: 'Just keep on riding, mister. I don't aim to give you any more warning. The next bullet will be in your head.'

With an effort, he eased himself back upright in the saddle, fighting for consciousness. There was a dull ache beginning to spread into his shoulder and he could feel a warm stickiness on his shirt and chest and knew that he had opened the wound once more. He waited tensely for the woman to come out. There was a faint, uncomfortable feeling in the pit of his stomach as he sat there, for it was impossible to tell what a woman with a rifle in her hands might do, especially when she was acting in defence of her home. There was something happening around this territory, something bad, but he did not know what it was and with the endless throbbing at the back of his temples, making it difficult for him to focus properly, his mind refused to think things out.

The woman stepped out on to the porch, the rifle held in firm hands, levelled on his chest, her finger still on the trig-

ger. She obviously needed little tempting to shoot. Bart stared
at her in surprise for a moment. She was a tall woman, in her
late twenties, he guessed, with hair long and flowing, the
colour of corn at the time of scything, a beautiful face, now
tight with determination. Her eyes were narrowed against the
red rays of the rising sun and she jerked the gun up sharply
as he moved weakly in the saddle.

'You heard what I said, stranger. Get moving. We don't
want men like you around here. You've had it your way long
enough. Now we're getting ready to fight. Seems like you
didn't heed our warning.'

'I don't know what's been happening around here,
ma'am,' he began slowly, lifting his hands so that she might
see he did not carry them near his guns. 'But I only came
here to get help. I—'

He swayed forward in the saddle as a fresh spasm of pain
lanced through his shoulder. The blood on his shirt showed
clearly now as he swayed back for a moment. Through
blurred eyes, he saw the rifle barrel suddenly waver, then
lower, as the woman started forward. That was almost all that
he saw. His last glimpse of her before he finally lost consciousness and slid to the ground was of her hurrying forward, the
rifle leaning against the post of the porch.

He came to some time later with the unaccustomed feel of
cool, clean sheets next to his body. With an effort, he forced
his eyes open, screwing them up in the harsh glare of sunlight
that came pouring in through the half-open windows of the
small room. He was in a bed close to the wall and for a long
moment, memory fought to return to his dulled mind. Then
he remembered riding up to the small homestead, recalled
the slim, tall woman with the hair the colour of corn who had
held the rifle on him and told him to keep riding. He tried to
move his body, to sit up in the bed, but there was still a great
weakness in him and his shoulder was throbbing painfully.
Swallowing, he lay back and looked up at the ceiling for a

long moment, wondering where the woman was and what she was doing, trying to figure out, above all, how he had come to be there. There was a faint sound outside the house, then a door opened and closed in the distance. He turned his head as the door of the room opened, saw the woman framed in the opening. She carried bandages in her hands and a bowl of water that steamed. Coming forward, she placed the water and bandages on the small table at the side of the bed, then glanced down at him, a faint smile on her features.

'I see you've finally come round, stranger.' She dipped her fingers into the water. 'I'd better take a look at that shoulder of yours. You've been pretty badly shot up. The slug is still there, I'm afraid. And it isn't going to be easy getting it out.'

'How did I get in here?' Bart asked quietly. 'The last I remember I was on the horse outside in the courtyard.'

'That's right. I thought you were one of Zena Clayburne's riders. You looked like one when I first saw you and I couldn't take any chances.' She wrung out the cloth and began to strip away the bandages from his shoulder, exposing the circular, purple-edged hole where the heavy calibre bullet had smashed into his flesh. 'I dragged you here and put you to bed. You were unconscious and I couldn't possibly have left you out there.'

He bit his lower lip as pain stabbed through his body, then leaned back on the pillow. 'I haven't thanked you yet for what you've already done for me,' he said slowly, 'I don't even know your name. Mine's Shannon. Bart Shannon.'

'Pleased to know you, Bart.' Her voice was calm and grave. 'I'm Tess Guthrie. My father and brother work this ranch between them, but both are away right now, rounding up the strays. We've lost quite a few head of cattle lately and we have to bring them in as quickly as we can, or they'll all be rustled.'

Bart's mouth tightened. A few little facts were now beginning to slot themselves into place in his mind. He saw the look on the girl's face and gave a slight nod. 'You figured I might be one of these rustlers?'

31

'It looked that way. We don't usually get many callers here unless they have orders to burn or pillage. This isn't a happy country, Bart. If you stay here for long, you'll soon realize that. Almost every day, some ranch is razed to the ground, or cattle are rustled from the outlying hills and driven north to the Clayburne spread. Trouble is that we haven't been able to prove anything so far, and even if we do, nobody will back us against her. Even the sheriff is in cahoots with her, so there ain't no use appealing to him for help.'

Bart wrinkled his brows, looked straight at her. He could see the pride which showed in every line of her, and also the hurt and worry which lay at the back of her eyes and in the faint lines of strain just visible on her regular features. A darkness showed faintly under the grey eyes, like that of a woman who knew what it was to shed tears and then to have to forget them and fight against something which threatened to break and destroy her whole life. 'I'm not one of those rustlers,' he said gently. 'But I do have a mission here. These killers ambushed our herd as we were crossing the river some fifty miles away to the south-east in the Badlands. They were lying in wait for us on this side of the river, obviously knew exactly where to wait for us.'

'You lost all of your cattle?' Her eyes flicked over him, then went to the hole in his shoulder. She picked up the long forceps and held them steadily in her right hand for a moment. 'I'd like to leave this until my brother or father get here,' she explained softly. 'But there's no way of telling how long that might be and that slug will have to come out soon. No doctor within calling distance either, I'm afraid. Think you can take it, Bart? There's a drink of whiskey there if you feel like it.'

'Go ahead with what you have to do,' he told her. 'Can't be much worse than what I suffered riding across that desert yesterday. And as you say, it's got to come out as soon as possible.'

'Just lie back and try not to talk until it's over,' she told

32

him firmly, pressing him back against the pillows. 'This is going to hurt.' She waited until he had gulped down a couple of mouthfuls of the neat whiskey, coughing as the raw liquor hit the back of his throat, then went down into his stomach where it expanded into a cloud of hazy warmth.

'OK. Go ahead.' He gritted his teeth and twisted his head on to one side. There was a moment when nothing happened, then he felt the girl start to probe for the bullet and the sweat popped out on to his face and started to run down his cheeks where it dripped off on to the sheet under him. The muscles of his neck corded and tightened as he clamped his teeth still tighter together in his mouth. Fire blazed through flesh and bone as she probed deeper. The bullet had hit the bone, but fortunately had not shattered it, rather it had glanced off it and ploughed a little more deeply into his flesh than it would normally have done.

The girl paused a little while later, and sat back in the chair. There were beads of perspiration on her face too now, but her hand, he noticed, was still as steady as before. God, but she had nerve, he thought sharply, in spite of the pain. There were not many women who would attempt anything like this alone, with the nearest medical help many miles away.

'I haven't managed to get it out yet,' she said, almost as an apology. 'It seems to have penetrated quite deeply into the flesh.' She dabbed more hot water on to it, wiping away the blood.

'You're doing fine,' he told her. He took another gulp of the raw whiskey and sank back. There was still a feeling of dizziness but the pain in his shoulder forced him awake. Tess Guthrie started again, the metal probe working into the wound, touching raw flesh, hurting as she knew it would, knowing that she had to go on now that she had committed herself. Bart clenched his teeth tightly and gripped the metal sides of the bed. Then he felt something move inside the wound, heard the woman's deep exhalation of breath and a moment later, there was a dull metallic thud as the slug dropped on to the wooden table.

'There.' She murmured the word softly. 'Now I'll clean it up and bandage it properly. Another week or so and you should be on your feet again. But I doubt whether you'll be able to use that hand for gunplay quite so soon.'

He shot her a quick, probing glance. 'How did you know about that?' he asked tightly.

She gave a quick nod. 'I noticed the guns you were wearing when you rode in. Those were gunman's weapons. They looked as though they had been used often in the past. And you seemed like a man with vengeance on your mind.'

'Perhaps you're right.' He nodded. 'As for the guns, I took them from one of the men who was killed during that rustling attack. Mine were lost somewhere in the bluffs when one of those hired killers jumped me.'

'And the vengeance?' She raised the delicate brows. 'What about that? Is that part true?'

He paused for a long moment, deliberately hesitant, wondering how much he dared tell this woman. She had spoken of someone behind a well-run rustling organization and it seemed logical to assume that they were one and the same person as the one he was seeking.

'Yes, it's true,' he admitted eventually. 'Those men killed all of my companions when they rustled that herd. They did it deliberately and in cold blood. In particular, they killed the best friend I ever had, a man named Dodson. In his last moments, he made me swear that I would hunt down his killers, and whoever was at the back of them, and destroy them all. That, I intend to do, even if it takes me the rest of my life.'

The girl checked a sudden retort. She sat in the tall, high-backed chair and eyed him strangely for a moment before saying: 'I heard a lot of cattle moving through the far end of the valley during the early part of the night. They could have heen your herd. If they were, you'll be too late to prove anything by the time that you're fit and well enough to get around. They'll have every single brand changed by then and you can't go against that evidence. Some have tried it in the past, but they haven't got anywhere; not with Sheriff Jason running things in Cochita City.'

'He's in with the rustlers, I gather.'

She nodded. 'I can tell that you're a real stranger in these parts. It won't be easy for you to understand what has happened around here during the past six or seven years. Before that time, this was a thriving little community, growing quite rapidly, with plenty of good grazing land to be had for raising cattle. There was law and order in the town and we had little trouble from any renegades or outlaws. They seemed to steer clear of us so long as Sheriff Keene was alive. When he was killed, it seemed to be the end of everything as far as we were concerned.'

'I don't follow you, Tess,' Bart said quietly, lying back on the pillow now that the fresh, clean bandages were in place.

The girl's tone was lifeless as she went on: 'There's no evidence to show that it was one of Zena Clayburne's killers who shot down Sheriff Keene in the back, but we have our own ideas on that score.' Bitterness crept into her tone. 'She comes from an aristocratic family back east and from the beginning she was determined that she would be the richest and most powerful landowner in the whole of the territory. She bought the Double-Y spread north of Cochita City and began to build up a herd of beef cattle. Then she put Clem Jason into office as sheriff in Cochita City and brought in her own hands to run the place. There was no law and order after that. And it was about that time, four years ago. that the rustling started along the trails. A few cattle here, thirty head there. Small rustlings in the beginning, but gradually, whole herds were being taken by outlaws and the sheriff seemed unable to prevent it.'

Bart nodded, his lips tight. He could guess the rest of the story, but he waited for Tess to tell it in her own words.

'It wasn't long before she tried to buy out some of the smaller ranch owners around town. When they refused to sell out to her at her price, outlaws raided the homesteads and ranches, burned barns to the ground, rustled cattle, ruined crops. If that didn't work, she made sure that any loans advanced by the bank, were called in on the day they were due and no extensions were allowed.'

'I see.' It was the same old story throughout the West whenever a powerful and completely unscrupulous person tried to set himself, or herself, up above the others. They would stop at nothing to gain their own ends and in the last analysis, even the law would be perverted to bring this about. 'And you think that these are the same men who rustled our herd back there?'

'I'd say there was no doubt about it. But single-handed, you'll be able to prove nothing, even if you stay alive. And if they discover that you are alive, that you're a witness against them, your life will be worth absolutely nothing. Believe me, I know what I'm talking about. They're all born killers.'

'Then why don't all of the decent men in the territory band together to drive her out? If you don't, she'll take you one by one and there'll be nothing to stop her.'

'They're all afraid of her.' Scorn tinged her voice as she rose to her feet and walked over to the window, staring out into the courtyard. 'If only we could get rid of Jason and put a real man in his place, a man who could stand up to them and bring some law into the town.'

'Even if you kill this man, do you think they'll stand by while you put another man into his place?'

Tess whirled, her face hard. 'It's the only chance we've got, unless you have any better ideas.'

36

He sighed and shook his head, leaning deeper into the pillow.

It was ten days later before the wound in his shoulder had healed enough to allow Bart Shannon to get up and move around. Three days after he had arrived there, Tess's father and her brother Jed returned to the small ranch. They had listened carefully while Tess explained to them all that had happened, but apart from a few questions concerning the herd itself, their original destination and the number of head in it, they did not seem inclined to question him further, accepting his word for everything that had occurred.

On the tenth day, he stood in the small courtyard, drawing the cool air down into his lungs, working the muscles of his shoulder in an attempt to get them back into shape, standing in the centre of the courtyard, his right hand dropping methodically and evenly towards the gun in its holster, jerking it out and up in a smooth, easy draw, the hammer clicking loudly and ominously on an empty cartridge. Some day, he told himself fiercely, the men who had attacked the herding party would stand in front of that gun, and he would shoot them down in cold blood as they had shot his companions.

He pulled his lips back thinly as he practised the draw. His arm was still stiff and sore but he forced it to work, sliding the heavy gun out of its leather holster time and time again, checking himself, co-ordinating every single movement until they flowed into a smooth motion.

Clem Guthrie came over from the house and stood for a moment, eyeing him up and down. The sunlight etched shadows over his grizzled features. He nodded slowly as Bart paused, then turned to face him.

'I'd sure hate to be the man in front of that gun when you meet up with him, son,' he drawled heavily. 'You reckon you know where to find him?'

'Probably in Cochita City,' muttered Bart harshly. 'If not, I'll just have to keep on riding until I do find him. And when I do, then I'm pretty certain that I'll find the others with him.'

Guthrie nodded. 'Could be that you're right. Tess told me what happened and how you came to be here. This ain't the first time a herd has been bushwhacked on the trail, but mostly they've attacked the northern trail. How come you were riding herd so far south? Bad country down that direction. You could have lost half of those cattle before you reached water, after leaving the river.'

'I know. But Dodson had heard of these outlaw gangs while we were further back east and he figured that, perhaps, if we cut south, we might manage to slip through. Seems we were wrong on all counts.'

'They have their ways of knowing when a rich herd is passing through and the trail they'll take. Reckon you were lucky to get that far, but they probably figured you might have a herd of that size well guarded and they weren't taking any chances on getting more men killed than they had to.' The other rolled himself a smoke, running the tip of his tongue along the paper, then thrusting the cigarette between his lips, lighting it and inhaling deeply. He blew smoke into the air.

'What d'yuh figger on doing now? Riding into Cochita City and trying to find this man you're looking for?' He eyed Bart steadily. 'You're fast, I'll admit that but that wound has slowed you up. No idea myself what you were like before you got that bullet in your shoulder, but I reckon you were a mite faster than you are now. Reckon that you're ready to go in there looking for a gun-fight?'

'No time like the present,' said Bart shortly. 'Besides, I need evidence about that herd. Tess reckons they'll have switched brands by now, but there were over four thousand head and it would take them a long time to do that. I may be able to find something definite if I snoop around long enough.'

The other looked at him for a moment, then shook his head. 'You won't live that long if you start asking the wrong kind of questions in Cochita City. Take my word for that. Zena Clayburne has eyes and ears everywhere. She'd know you were there within an hour of you hitting town.'

'Could be that I'd be going about it the wrong way then. Perhaps I ought to go and have a talk with Zena Clayburne. Figure she ought to know all of the answers to the questions that've been worrying me.'

'You ain't serious, son.' For a moment, the older man looked startled. 'Now that's fool talk. You'd never leave that ranch alive.'

But Bart wasn't listening. There was the sound of a horseman approaching from the distance. He felt a sudden wave of apprehension pass through him as he looked up, past the older man, to where Jed Guthrie rode into the courtyard. The dust was heavy on his jacket, clinging to his legs, as he swung himself out of the saddle.

'Where have you been, Jed?' asked the older man tightly.

The other's face was sullen and bore a strange look as he came forward, staring straight at Bart. He thinned his lips and his right hand hovered an inch above the gun in its holster. 'That ain't the point now,' he said sharply. 'Ask this *hombre* where he was when that herd was rustled near the river. Go on, ask him and let's see that we get some straight talk this time. Must admit that he even had me fooled at first with his talk of being shot up by rustlers.'

Bart stiffened. He levelled his gaze with the other's, watching the man's eyes, knowing that something had happened, but unsure what it was that had brought about this sudden change in the other's attitude.

'Just what is all this about, Jed?' demanded his father tightly. He flicked his gaze from Bart to his son and then back again. 'Where've you been, coming along with fool questions like that?'

'I've been in town for the past hour, trying to get a lead on what really happened to that herd,' rasped Jed harshly. His hand remained in position just over the butt of the gun in its holster, as if he expected to have to go for it at any moment. 'Seems this *hombre* weren't telling the truth when he came here.' His voice held an odd edge of anger – and something else too, perhaps a little fear at the back of it, decided Bart. 'Wouldn't be too difficult to make Tess believe you, I suppose. Probably you figured that you'd be well away from here before anyone went into town and learned the truth about you.'

'And just what is the truth?' asked the older Guthrie quietly.

'I'll tell you,' gritted his son. 'There's plenty of talk in town about that raid on the herd. Sure, it seems Zena Clayburne is at the back of it as always, but nobody can prove anything and Sheriff Jason ain't doing any talking about that. Only thing he knows, is that one of those polecats managed to get away after the gunplay, but he was shot in the shoulder when he tried to make his get-away over the bluffs. They reckon that he pitched about thirty feet down the side of the bluff, but was lucky enough to get away with his life.' His eyes flicked back to Bart. 'Seem to recall that your body was covered with bruises,' he said thinly. 'You don't get marks like that in a gunfight – not unless you fall down the face of the bluffs. There's a warrant been sworn out by Jason for your arrest and I reckon I beat that posse by about ten minutes, riding hard in this direction.'

So that was it! Bart drew in a deep breath. This was something that he hadn't bargained for when he had come here; that Zena Clayburne would try to get rid of him this way. Somehow, she must have learned that an injured man had arrived at the Guthrie homestead and been taken in by Tess. A man who represented a very real menace as far as this ambitious and ruthless woman was concerned, a man who had to be removed as quickly as possible, and if it were possible to use the law for that end, then why not do so. He ought to have foreseen this possibility, he told himself fiercely, especially after Tess had told him of how Jason was in the pay of Zena Clayburne. She would not want to go against the whole town by having him strung up from the most convenient tree unless she could make out that he was in cahoots with these outlaws and rustlers. And his hanging like this would be a double-edged weapon as far as she was concerned. For there was no doubt that she would exploit this as far as she could, spreading the word around that she intended to hang every outlaw run to earth by Sheriff Jason and his posse. That, in itself, would be enough to divert suspicion from her for some time to come.

He drew himself upright, feet wide spread, arms swinging loose. Turning, he stared straight at Jed Guthrie. 'I don't know what lies this Clayburne woman has been spreading about me around Cochita City,' he said flatly. 'But I was riding herd with Matt Dodson and as far as I know, I was the only one of that trail crew who was left alive when those killers took off with the herd. I followed them across the desert after swearing that I would kill them for what they did. You can believe that or not as you like. But you're a fool if you can't see that she's deliberately framed me for this so that she can get rid of me.'

'So you say now,' sneered Jed.

'At least you rode in ahead of that posse to warn me,' Bart pointed out quietly. 'That must mean you have some doubt about my guilt.'

Jed Guthrie shook his head slowly. 'No doubt at all. I came out here first to take you in myself. There's two thousand dollars reward for your capture, offered by Miss Clayburne – dead or alive.'

Bart's eyes snapped dangerously. 'I wouldn't try it if I were you,' he said ominously. 'I'm faster than you are, even with this shoulder. And I don't want to have to shoot you down, not after all that your sister and father have done for me while I've been here.'

Jed's eyes met his, alive with challenge. But he hesitated. He had seen Bart in action, and that alone made him pause. For a long moment, there was silence, then the older man said: 'I think you're wrong, Jed. Keep your hand away from that gun of yours. That ain't going to solve anything. Believe me, I know Zena Clayburne and this is the kind of thing she would do. I don't reckon she would offer two thousand dollars reward money for a man dead or alive, unless she knew that she had something to fear from him. If Bart here was the killer she's trying to make him seem, then she'd have him on her payroll before nightfall.'

Jed's gaze wavered. Then he lowered his right hand until it hung loosely at his side. 'I'm still not sure,' he said sullenly. 'If he is a killer, I say we ought to give him up to the sheriff. He'll be here in less than ten minutes.'

'You reckon he was riding straight for here?'

'Didn't seem much doubt about it from the trail he took. Reckon they must have heard he was here and decided to ride out to get him.'

The older man turned quickly. 'You'll have to get away,' he said urgently. 'Ride for the hills to the south. Plenty of places there where you can hide out for a coupla days. Once things cool off here, we'll try to get word to you and then it might be safe enough for you to return. But hurry. If they know that you came here, nothing is going to stop them and you'll have to get clear of the ranch before they surround the place.'

'No time for that,' snapped Jed swiftly. 'Here they come.' He pointed to the north.

Bart glanced up swiftly. The closely-packed bunch of riders was just visible, spurring their horses along the narrow trail which wound around the lee of the hill. Bart estimated that there were at least a score of them, men who intended to take no chances. His keen-eyed gaze flicked around the courtyard, then back to the hills to the south. No way of escape in that direction, he reflected bitterly. The posse would spot him immediately he tried to make a run for it. He could stand his ground, of course, and try to shoot it out with them when they arrived, but what chance did one man have against twenty?

CHAPTER III

JAILBREAK!

Sheriff Jason was a big, burly man with a florid face that streamed with sweat as he sat his horse and stared down at Bart. The rest of the men in the posse were spread out around the small courtyard, some with rifles over the pommels of their saddles, all wary, ready to shoot if he made the slightest move towards the guns slung low at his waist. A thick moustache gave a sinister cast to Jason's face and he had a way of talking which left no doubt that he wouldn't hesitate to order his men to shoot if it served his purpose to bring in Bart dead, rather than alive.

'I'm sure glad you didn't make a try for those guns of yours when we rode in,' he said thickly. 'I don't like gunplay, least-ways not when it can be avoided. There's a warrant out for your arrest on a charge of rustling and murder. Now, do you aim to come along quietly with us back to town, or do we have to take you the hard way.'

'You know that I wasn't in that rustling party, Sheriff,' Bart said thinly. He moved forward a couple of paces. 'I'd like to know who swore out that warrant. Was it Zena Clayburne?'

For a second, the other's eyes narrowed to mere slits in his puffy face. Then he shrugged. 'Don't know how you knew that, stranger,' he muttered. 'But it was Miss Clayburne.'

Bart raised his brows slightly. 'Any idea how she came to know I was with those killers, Sheriff?' There was a deliberate hard edge to his voice. 'Reckon it's true that I can't prove anything of what I say – not when all of my companions were killed in the gunfight. Only reason I'm not resisting is that I don't want any of these folk here to get killed just on account of me.'

Guthrie spoke up a moment later, before Bart could go on: 'You know that you ain't got any evidence against Bart, Sheriff,' he snapped. 'This is all a frame put up by Zena Clayburne. She's in this rustling business up to her pretty neck and you know it. She has to get rid of Bart because he's the only man living who can identify those men who rustled the herd.'

Jason swung on the other, holding himself upright in the saddle. For a moment, Bart had the impression that he intended to go for his gun, and his own hands dropped a little towards his sides, ready to shoot it out if the sheriff made any move like that. Abruptly, Jason relaxed and barked a harsh laugh. 'You're mad, Guthrie.' He leaned forward over the neck of his sorrel. 'But I'm warning you, here and now. Any more talk like that and I'll see to it that Miss Clayburne knows. Perhaps she might swear out a warrant for your arrest too.'

'On what charge?' demanded the other thinly, 'Another trumped up murder charge against me? You can't hope to kill off every man in Cochita City. Sooner or later, they're going to start asking themselves questions about Miss Clayburne and the way her herd seems to be growing all the time. Funny there ain't been no rustling on her spread.' He added the last words meaningly.

'Just keep your mouth closed around here,' repeated Jason.' He lifted his head, looked at Bart. 'All right, mister. Get on your horse and we'll ride outa here. Don't make any funny moves or you might find that one of my men has an itchy finger. Better drop those guns of yours real slow.'

Bart shrugged. He pulled the guns from their holsters, held them loosely in his hands, aware that every man in the courtyard had his eyes on him, waiting to see if he intended to use them, or obey Jason. He was on the point of releasing his hold on them when there came a sudden interruption from the ranch. Tess Guthrie's voice, clear and loud, said suddenly. 'Just sit quite still, Jason, or you'll he the first to die. Tell those coyotes with you to let their weapons fall or you'll be the first to get a bullet.'

Bart saw the abruptly changing expression on the sheriff's florid features. For a moment, he contemplated going for his horse while Tess held the others there with the rifle trained on them. Then he decided against it, as Jason said throatily: 'Don't be a fool, Miss Guthrie. If he gets on that horse and rides out of here, we'll see to it that there isn't a building left standing on this land. You'll be an accessory to murder helping him.'

'He's right, Tess,' said Bart slowly. 'It's no use anyway. Mebbe if the townsfolk in Cochita City know what's really going on they might decide to do something and take the law into their own hands.'

'Do you honestly think that Jason and Zena Clayburne will allow you to get a fair trial, Bart?' There was a note of scorn in Tess's voice. The rifle was still trained steadily on Jason's back. 'You'll be lucky if you get into town alive. Probably they'll decide to string you up from a convenient tree somewhere along the trail back. They'll claim that you tried to make a break for it and they had to kill you.'

'Guess that's a chance I'll have to take.' He let his guns drop to the ground. 'Put that rifle away, Tess. He means every word that he says about burning this place to the ground.'

Reluctantly, she lowered the rifle, then stepped back quickly into the house. Jason nodded slowly. 'Now you're showing some sense, mister,' he said thickly. He waited until his men had picked up their weapons, then motioned Bart towards the waiting mount. Slowly, Bart swung himself up

46

into the saddle. There was a tight tenseness in him that threatened to crowd out all other thoughts in his mind and it was only with a conscious mental effort that ne managed to bring his spinning mind under control. As he sat in the saddle, looking down at Guthrie, he said quietly: 'If I don't get into Cochita City alive, I reckon you'll know what to do,' he gave a quick nod towards the sheriff but the other merely motioned angrily with his rifle.

'Get moving,' he said savagely. 'You'll get a heap more than those men you killed with that herd. A chance to clear your name.'

The jailhouse was at the north end of the town where the main street ended and the foothills began. An occasional cottonwood gave a little shade in the harsh glare of the noon sun and half a mile away, where the hills climbed towards the blue sky, there were patches of deep green which spoke of lush pastures where cattle could be raised, of fertile hidden valleys and slopes. Here, he guessed, would be the spread which belonged to Zena Clayburne. Even as he rode along the hard, dusty, sun-glaring street, with the posse riding on either side of him, and men and women watching curiously from the boardwalk, he wondered about this woman who had come here from back east and was now the richest and most powerful person in the whole of this territory.

She seemed to be the kind of person who kept herself in the background, preferring to let men like Jason do the dirty work for her. He reined his mount in front of the jailhouse, swung himself down as the other men crowded him, their rifles ready. Even though he was unarmed, they meant to take no chances. Jason went inside and one of the men prodded Bart in the small of the back with the barrel of his rifle, thrusting him forward.

'Inside,' he snapped. We won't keep you waiting in jail fer long. Justice is swift in Cochita City. Judge ought to be here day after tomorrow.'

'Seems to me that you're pretty sure I was with those killers,' said Bart harshly, as he stumbled forward. Behind him, he could pick out some of the conversation in the crowd which had gathered outside the jailhouse. There were angry murmurs and although he could only pick out scattered snatches of the conversation, echoed by a scattering of voices, several calling on the sheriff to bring him back out of the building, to lynch him there and then, There were some trouble-makers in the crowd, he reflected, probably placed there on purpose, to stir up the others, but from what he had seen, he knew that the majority of people out there in the street were still unsure of his guilt.

As the door of the cell closed behind him, Jason said tightly: 'Seems those folk out there are getting themselves worked up about you. You'd better keep quiet in there, or they may decide to take things into their own hands and if they do, there ain't much I could do about it. I've only three deputies here to take care of the prisoners and I don't want any trouble.'

'So you'd turn me over to them without hesitation. Is that it, Sheriff?'

'If you're still alive when the circuit judge arrives the day after tomorrow, you'll get your trial,' snapped the sheriff, almost as if he had not heard the question. 'In the meantime, I'd advise you not to make any trouble.' He turned on his heel and walked off along the narrow passage. Bart took a quick glance around the cell, then sat down on the hard bunk in the corner. There was a solitary window, less than a foot square, with four iron bars set in it. He guessed that it looked out on to the small alley at the side of the jailhouse and through it, he could still hear the angry murmur of the crowd in the main street. Once or twice, there was a sound of a gun being fired, the sharp echoes clearly heard. But after a while, the crowd seemed to have dispersed and there was a hot silence outside.

Lying down on the hard bunk, he clasped his hands

behind his head and stared up at the ceiling, trying to think things out. There seemed little doubt that Jason intended to have him killed before the circuit judge did reach Cochita City. Already, the trouble-makers, possibly Zena Clayburne's men, would be mingling with the crowds in the saloons, stirring up trouble, spreading the word that he had been responsible for the deaths of several good and decent men in the herding party. He lay quietly, unmoving, acutely conscious of how helpless he was here. If the mob did attack the jailhouse, demanding that he should he taken out and lynched, Jason would do nothing to prevent it. And he was unarmed and unable to resist the mob. For the first time, he began to doubt the wisdom of having agreed to go with these men in the first place. Had it not been for the inescapable fact that Jason would certainly have carried out his threat of destroying the Guthrie place, he would have taken his chance when it had been presented to him. By now, he debated, he could have been well away into the hills far to the south, out of reach of Jason and Zena Clayburne.

One of the deputies came with a tray full of food and a mug of hot, weak coffee, two hours later, opening the door warily, keeping one hand close to the gun in its holster. His eyes never left Bart's face as he placed the food in the middle of the floor, then backed away, locking the door behind him.

As the other stood outside in the passage, Bart said quietly; 'Do they figure on lynching me tonight, before the judge gets here?'

The deputy licked his lips drily. He seemed ill at ease. 'You ain't liked in this town,' he said finally. 'Word has got around that you were with that outlaw band who waylaid and ambushed the herd south of here ten days ago. Seems we were wrong about Miss Clayburne. Most of us used to figure that she was behind this rustling and killing. Don't seem likely now. She wouldn't let one of her own hands die in jail like this.'

'Don't suppose it's any use telling you that I wasn't with

49

those outlaws at all, that I was the only one of that herding party left alive,' said Bart slowly, flatly.

The man shook his head quickly, a trifle nervously. He kept glancing over his shoulder in the direction of the end of the passage as if expecting the mob to break in at any moment and take Bart away. 'We figured you might try to wriggle out of it like that. The sheriff is out there now, trying to calm these folk down, but it ain't goin' to be easy. There are a lot of roughnecks in town tonight and they're trying to stir up trouble in the saloons. Big party of them over the street, fifty yards away. If they do try to take the law into their own hands, I don't want to be around here when they come for you.'

'So you intend to run out and leave me to them.' It was more of a statement than a question. Bart glared at the other as he picked up the plate. 'Seems to me that everybody has made up their minds about me already. I thought that even here a man was innocent until they proved him guilty.'

There was a sullen mutter of sound from somewhere outside. Bart threw a swift glance towards the window that looked out upon the sky and saw, with a faint sense of surprise, that it was already dark. By now, the trouble-makers would have plied most of the decent citizens of Cochita City with drink and they would be ready to believe anything. And if he guessed right at Sheriff Jason's real motives, he knew that the other would be out there trying to stir folk up a little more, rather than attempting to calm them down. He would have his orders too from Zena Clayburne. Make sure that Bart Shannon was not alive the next morning, but don't make it too obvious that he died without a fair trial.

The angry muttering outside grew louder, seemed to be coming nearer. Out of the corner of his eye, Bart saw the other glance nervously along the passage, grip the bars of the cell for a moment with fingers that showed white with the pressure he was exerting, then he turned swiftly on his heel and went quickly along the passage, out of sight. He was running away, thought Bart tightly; getting out of the jail-house while he had a whole skin. In their present mood, the crowd might not stop at shooting a deputy if they figured that he would try to stop them from getting the man they intended to kill.

He could hear the individual voices now, at the front of the jail. A man called loudly: 'I've got a rope. I say we go in there and get him. Evidently Jason ain't going to turn him over to us.'

'Now listen to me, men.' Jason's thick voice, raised above the others. 'I know exactly how you feel. We've got a cold-blooded killer locked up in there. He's the only one we've caught so far of the gang that jumped this herd, but he still has the right to a fair trial. The judge will be here in less than forty-eight hours and if he's guilty, then the law will hang him. Take my word for it.'

The silence that followed these words had a rising tension in it that Bart could sense, even from inside the jail. In his mind's eye, he could visualize the stocky figure of the sheriff standing on the steps of the jailhouse, facing the crowd, possibly with his rifle held loosely in his hands, making a pretence of preventing them from going in and fetching out his prisoner, but knowing all the time that they would not listen to him.

'Just get out of the way,' yelled a hoarse voice. 'We've done with listening to words. Stand on one side, Sheriff, and we'll take over now. I say we ought to string him up right now, and save ourselves the expense of a trial. He's as guilty as hell. You know that as well as we do, Sheriff.'

'Mebbe he is and mebbe he isn't.' Jason was playing his part well. This was perhaps the biggest chance he would get to try to put over to the townsfolk that he was not in Zena Clayburne's pay and he was making the most of it. 'But he's still entitled to a trial. If he's guilty, then he'll hang. You can take my word for that.'

'Mebbe we're tired of waiting, Sheriff,' yelled another

51

voice. 'Cut the palaver and get him out here. If'n you don't, then we'll come in and get him, so don't make things any harder on yourself than you have to. We don't aim to stand around waiting for the law to get to the point of hanging this killer.'

There were harsh shouts at this remark. The crowd's rumble grew louder and more insistent. Bart got up and moved closer to the door, trying to peer along the dark corridor. It was impossible to make out the shape of the deputy who had hurried along it a few moments earlier. By now, Bart reflected, he would be outside in the street, probably joining the mob who wanted to lynch him. He looked about him quickly, knowing what his fate would be once the crowd laid hands on him. The trouble-makers had done their job only too well; and plenty of whiskey had helped to sway any doubters on to their side.

'Bart!'

He whirled at the whispered sound, staring about him for a long moment, before he made out the face at the barred window. Swiftly, he went forward, looked out in surprise.

'Tess! What in God's name are you doing there. Better get out of town before the crowd move in. They're aiming to string me up and Jason ain't going to do much to stop 'em.'

'Mebbe not, but we are.' There was a note of grim determination in the girl's voice. She thrust something in to him between the bars. It was a loaded Colt. He felt its cold, reassuring weight in his hand. He was still not out of danger yet, even though no longer unarmed. There was only one way out of the jailhouse, so far as he knew, and that led out on to the main street of Cochita City, where the crowd was lying in wait for him, growing more and more impatient as the seconds ticked away. He did not stand an earthly chance of fighting all of them, even with the gun.

'What do you intend to do?' he hissed. 'There are most of the townsfolk out front, ready to break in at any moment and that's the only way out of here.'

'Could be there'll be another exit soon.' She turned, said something to someone standing a little distance behind her. Over her shoulder, Bart could just make out the stocky figure of her father and just beyond him, three horses, waiting in the shadows of the narrow alley. It had not been difficult for them to reach this spot unseen and unheard. All of the town seemed to be gathered in the main street and they had obviously ridden in from the north, skirting the town and coming down from the hills. But how they intended to get him out of the jail, he still did not know.

Old Ned Guthrie came forward, a lariat in his hand. He gave Bart a quick nod, then slipped the end of the strong rope through the barred window, around three of the bars, before leading it out again and fashioning a running noose on the end. Bart got the idea then, but it still didn't look as though it would work. The walls of the jail seemed strongly built and the iron bars were set deeply in the window.

The girl said swiftly, in a rush of words. 'These bars may look strong, like the wall around the window, but it's far weaker than it looks. When it does come away, get out as quickly as you can, take the third horse and head for the hills to the north.'

'But what about you and your father?' he demanded. 'They'll know that you were the ones who helped me to escape.'

'Never mind that at the moment. I'll ride with you. There's an old cabin up there in the hills where you can hide out until we decide what to do next. I'll show you where it is, you'd never find it by yourself. My father will hold off these coyotes until we get well away. In the darkness, they'll never be able to follow our trail. Now get ready to move.'

Before he could protest, tell her that her scheme could not possibly work, she had gone back into the darkness to where her father was busy hitching the other end of the rope to the saddle horn of one of the horses. Bart glanced suddenly at the plaster. There was the grinding of stone moving on stone as the cracks widened and a whole irregular section of the wall began to move outward. He could not tell what it looked like from the outside, but from where he stood it seemed pretty thick and solid, and he doubted that it could be pulled out by the tug of a lariat and horse, no matter how strong they might be. But the girl and her father seemed to know what they were doing, had obviously had this planned for some time and for the moment, he was in their hands and had to go along with their idea if he was to stand any chance at all. He could hear the hoarse shouts of the men at the front of the jailhouse as they argued with the sheriff. But they wouldn't stay there and argue for long, he knew, and when their patience was exhausted, they would brush the sheriff aside and storm the jail, ready to drag him out and hang him from the nearest tree.

A moment later, there came a thunderous sound from the far end of the passage outside his cell. It echoed through the bars and he knew instantly what it was. Someone had brought along a battering ram and they were attacking the stout door. It would hold for a little while, he thought inwardly, but not for long. And once it gave way, it would be a matter of moments before they reached the cell. There was a desperate sense of urgency within him now. He saw Guthrie step back, glanced quickly in the direction of the barred window, then hit the horse hard across the rump. It jerked forward, the lariat took the strain, tautened, and held. Bart held his breath as the horse leapt forward again. There was a faint screech of protest from the bars as they moved slightly in their sockets. Behind him, the din of the mob grew louder, drowning out any sound from the cell. Another shuddering blow against the door and he thought he heard it begin to splinter under the onslaught.

Outside, in the narrow alley, the horse moved slowly, straining on the rope. Bart moved a little distance away from the wall, then stared. Long cracks began to appear in the wall of the cell around the barred window. Clumsily, awkwardly, the large section of the wall crashed down into the alley. Before the dust had settled, Bart had leapt through the opening, scratching his arms and legs on the bricks, out into the open, running swiftly to where the horse stood waiting. Even as he swung himself up into the saddle, he noticed that Tess had climbed on to hers and at that same moment, there came a loud, exultant yell from around the corner where the mob in the main street had finally succeeded in breaking down the door of the jail.

'Hurry,' snapped Guthrie. 'there's no time to lose. Head for the hills. I'll keep them here for as long as I can.'

His tone brooked no argument. Kicking spurs to the horse, Barty felt it bound forward with a surge of muscles, carrying him along the alley, and then out between two low, slant-roofed shacks and into open country. Tess rode beside him, her own mount keeping pace with his as they rode away from Cochita City, keeping north. As he rode, his mind seemed strangely empty. He tried to think back to what had happened eleven days before, at the river crossing, when he had seen all of his companions shot down in the hail of bullets that had swept over them. But even though it seemed to have been imprinted on his brain like an image of fire at the time, he found to his surprise that some of the details were beginning to fade slightly until he could only remember the look on Dodson's face as he lay dying, when he had made that promise to hunt down and destroy his killers.

They rode in silence for a long while, the cold air tugging at them. Behind them, there was as yet, no sign of pursuit. But by now Bart knew that his escape must have been discovered.

'We're very close to Zena Clayburne's spread,' called Tess as they rode down a steep slope. She threw an arm to her left to indicate the undulating ridges which bordered a wide stretch of prairie. 'This is the only place where we may run into trouble. If she has any of her men patrolling the fences, they could spot us and decide to investigate.'

They skirted the boundary fence, rode through deep gullies and then set their mounts to the hills. The chill night air made them shiver as they climbed higher among the rocks. The ground here was hard and treacherous and Bart realized now that Tess had been right; he would never have found his way along this trail without her. Out of the corner of his eye, he watched her as she rode, taking the lead. They were travelling more slowly now, all danger of pursuit forgotten. She held her head high, eyes searching the rocks ahead as the trail wound and twisted among them. Inwardly, he wondered again why she was doing this for him. From what he had heard in the past few days, anyone who tried to set themselves up against Zena Clayburne usually ended up by being killed or run out of the territory. He thought, once or twice, of asking her outright, then decided against it. If she wanted to tell him, she would do so in her own good time. At the moment, all that mattered was for him to get under cover, until he had made further plans. At the moment, he didn't know exactly what to do. Zena Clayburne seemed to have her spies everywhere and there was little doubt that Cochita City was full of her men. The law was on her side, run by her from behind the scenes and very few of the smaller ranchers would dare to come out openly on his side as Tess and her father had when they had ridden into town to break him out of the jail.

He wondered, with a grim amusement, what Jason was doing at that moment. The other had righteously tried to prevent him from being hanged out of hand, knowing that the mob would break into the jail anyway to carry out their threat; but now she would know that he had escaped, and that was something Jason would have to explain in person to Zena Clayburne. He did not envy Jason that particular task, if what he had heard about this woman was true. There would be no place in her outfit for bunglers and men who could not be trusted to carry out her orders implicitly.

Bart drew the collar of his jacket up higher about his

throat as the cold air which swept down the side of the hills swirled about him, chilling him to the bone. Still, they continued to climb. He looked about him with a renewed interest as the dawn began to brighten slowly in the east. It seemed incredible that anyone should have lived here and yet the girl had spoken of a cabin in the rocks where he could hide out for a few days. Probably some old, half-crazed prospector who had come up here in the hope of finding riches and had died a broken and disillusioned man. There had been many men like that in the days just following the Civil War, when men had fought to find a way back to the kind of life they had known before. The trouble was, he mused inwardly, that the war had also fired a kind of man who thrived on killing, a man who would do anything so long as the price was right. And it was this breed of man who fell in so readily with a person such as Zena Clayburne, a woman who wanted riches and power and who did not care how she got it, nor how many lives were destroyed because of it.

Tess led her mount around a sharply-angled bend in the rocks where the trail twisted away out of sight. He urged his own mount forward. In front of him, the trail widened suddenly into a wide clearing, bounded on all sides by tall, rearing pinnacles of rock. In the centre of the clearing was the cabin that the girl had spoken about. He eyed it curiously as they rode towards it, the peculiar stillness of the hills settling tensely around them, the weird echoes of the horses' hoofs chasing each other among the boulders and rocky walls.

He slid from the saddle in front of the cabin and stood beside the girl for a moment as she tethered the horse to the pole in front. The place looked as if it had not been lived in for years. It made an excellent hide-out. From here, it was possible to command a complete view of the countryside for miles around and it would be virtually impossible to be taken by surprise. He nodded to himself, satisfied.

'How come you know about this place?' he asked quietly, as they walked forward.

She smiled at him. 'I often used to come here when I was younger,' she said softly. 'I thought then that no one else knew about this place but me. It used to belong to an old miner they called Crazy Groot. He used to come up here for long spells at a time, hunting for gold among the rocks. Nobody used to bother him and when he died, the place was deserted. You ought to be safe here. I doubt whether Zena Clayburne knows that it exists.'

'And Jason. What about him?'

She pursed her lips. 'He may have heard of it. But even if he has, I doubt if he'll think about it if he decides to take a posse out after you. He figures that you're headed south, into the hills there. He won't get around to coming here for some time yet, until he's examined every other likely place.'

She pushed open the door and stepped inside with Bart close on her heels. There was a musty smell in the room which stung the back of his nostrils and his heels clattered hollowly on the wooden floor.

'What about food and water'?' He looked at the girl, her face etched with shadow in the faint light that filtered through the dusty window panes.

'I brought some food up this afternoon,' she explained. 'There's a well outside, fresh water. You won't go short on that.'

'You must have thought of everything,' he said, admiringly. He lowered himself into the chair at the rough table and eyed her closely. 'Tell me, why are you doing all of this? I suppose you realize that if Zena Clayburne gets wind of it, or Sheriff Jason, both you and your father are as good as dead.'

'I know.' There was a note of defiance in her voice and in the way she held her head high. 'But somebody has to take a stand against these killers, or the whole of the town will soon be in their hands, together with every ranch and spread in the territory.'

58

'But why me?'

'Isn't it obvious? You have the best reason in the world for fighting these men. They killed your companions and you've sworn to kill them. We're fighting them to prevent them from taking over the entire territory. Surely we can get together on this? If we stand and fight, some of the others might join in. It's the only way we'll ever defeat them. Otherwise, she'll just keep on bringing in more killers from back east, holding up more stages and rustling more herds. By now, there must be close on twenty thousand head of cattle on her spread. And four thousand of them belonged to you and the men who were riding with you. Doesn't that mean something to you?'

He nodded slowly. 'It means a lot,' he admitted. 'But there ain't no sense in going into this blindly. At the moment, as far as I can see, she holds all of the aces. You can't fight against a hand like that and hope to win. There's still that warrant out against me for murder and even though I'm not guilty, I can't prove it.'

'Then how do you figure we can do it?' She looked at him directly, her face tight. 'Because whatever we do, we have to move fast. If I know Jason, by now he'll have sworn in half of the town as a posse, decent citizens as well as the rough-necks.'

'First of all, I reckon you'd better get back to your ranch before you're missed,' said Bart quietly. 'If they discover you there, they may believe that you had nothing to do with my escape. In the meantime, I'll try to figure out something. Is there no one in town that you can trust?'

The girl thought for a long moment, then looked up quickly. 'You can trust Ben Wheeler, he's the editor of the local paper. He was a great friend of Sheriff Keene. He tried then to make out a charge of murder against one of Zena Clayburne's hired gunmen, but a rigged jury found him not guilty and after that there was nothing anybody could do. But even he can do little, I'm afraid. Every move he makes is reported back to her. He showed his hand once, when he figured he might be backed up by the local townsfolk. When they failed him, he never tried again. Besides, if he tries to print anything against her again, there won't be any local paper any more.'

'I think I understand.' Bart nodded. He rose to his feet. 'You'd better pull out before daylight. If they find you in this neck of the woods, it could make things difficult. Not only for me, but for you.'

When Tess had gone, Bart spent fifteen minutes finding his way around the place, checking every trail which led up to this small clearing, making certain that it would be impossible for anyone to take him by surprise. Then he went back into the cabin and broke out some biscuits from the pack which the girl had left there. As she had said, there was a spring in the clearing near the rocks, cool clear water gushing out into a small stream that bubbled off down the side of the rock face.

Checking the guns in his holsters, he went back into the cabin and stretched himself out on the hard, wooden bed in the corner of the single room. Now that the sun was up, the air inside the room began to heat up and he grew aware of the weariness in his body. There was the chance that they might try to sneak up on him while he slept and for one moment, he debated whether or not he ought to remain awake; then decided against it. The odds against them finding him during the next few hours were, if Tess was right, small. And he would be in better shape to put up a fight if he rested, than if he stayed awake through the heat of the day.

Lying on his back, he let his breath out slow and easy, forcing himself to relax. The loaded guns were placed within easy reach of his hands, ready for instant use should the necessity arise. But it was not needed. He slept for the whole of the morning and most of the afternoon. When he finally woke, his back stiff and sore with the hardness of the bed, the sun had passed its zenith and was dipping down towards the west, throwing long, dark shadows across the canyon. He got slowly to his feet, ran his fingers over the stubble on his chin. They rasped loudly and he shrugged as he went outside, took a drink of the cold water from the spring and threw a swift, all-encompassing glance around him. The ground shimmered in the quiet haze as the heat rose from it, but apart from that, nothing moved. He scanned the narrow trail where it wound down the hillside, among the rocks and out on to the plain. No movement there. Nothing to show that anyone from town had lit on his trail and had followed it. For the moment, he felt secure. He had time in which to think things out and try to come up with an answer.

There had to be something he could do, he told himself fiercely. He had two guns and he wasn't afraid to use them; and he knew some of the men he was hunting down; knew that their faces would never be forgotten as long as there was breath in his body. But how to get at them – that was the big problem. And more important still, how to get at Zena Clayburne. Sooner or later, he felt certain, he and she would come face to face – and he wanted that to be at a time and place of his choosing, not hers.

Unconsciously, he looked towards the northern horizon, where Tess had pointed out the Clayburne spread. Almost, it was as if he could see beyond the skyline and see the massed herd of cattle for which so many men had died. Zena Clayburne was there and her hired killers. Of a sudden, Bart had an idea that there might be a way in which to defeat these people, but it would mean taking a greater risk than he had ever taken before.

He turned the idea over in his mind, assessing all of the possibilities. The more he thought it over, the more likely it seemed it would work. First, he had to see Zena Clayburne. It was a mad thought that ran through his mind, but he had never been a man to back down when the trail got rough. And the last place that anyone would think of looking for him would be on the Clayburne spread.

61

The next morning, just after sun-up, he mounted his sorrel, and put it to the trail leading down out of the rocks, down on to the wide, open prairie, and let it cut across to the north until he reached the boundary fence which ran around the Clayburne spread. He paused for a long moment there, with his hand on the horse's neck, staring out over the wire into the stretching green pastures of lush feeding grass which lay beyond. There was a large herd in the distance, on the brow of a low hill, but from that distance, he could make out nothing of the brand. It might be the herd which had been stolen from them at the river. A herd with the brand altered by deft strokes of the branding iron. His eyes narrowed a little as he saw the men who rode the herd. Some of those men could be the killers he was searching for. At the moment, he did not want them to see him. It was doubtful if any of them, except one, would recognize him – and that exception was the big man who had fired at him, the man who still had his bullet in him, and had watched him fall over the edge of the bluff trail, seemingly to his death on the hard rock ground below.

Absently almost, he eased the heavy guns in their holsters, then felt along his right wrist where the long, slender-bladed knife was strapped tightly against his flesh. This time, he was taking no chances.

A few moments later, he found the entrance through the wire and put the horse through, on to the Clayburne spread. There was a wide trail that wound over the hill in the distance, a trail which he guessed would lead right up to the ranch itself. For an instant he paused, but only for a few seconds, then he rode forward through the tall, green grass.

CHAPTER IV

THE SHOWDOWN!

As he rode, Bart tried to make an estimate of the size of the spread. It seemed to stretch for many miles to the north and west of Cochita City, with its boundaries clear to the river which flowed north and south through the territory. It was good land. An experienced cowman himself, he recognized that instantly. A spread that could feed many thousand head of prime beef cattle. He experienced no difficulty in following the trail. It had evidently been used many times and an hour later, with the sun high in the heavens, he topped a long, high rise and found himself staring down into the length of a narrow valley, at the far end of which stood the ranch.

He reined his mount and sat in thoughtful silence for several moments, watching the place. The walls glinted white in the streaming sunlight and there were several barns and a large stockade to the east. From where he sat, he could just make out the figures of several men working in the stockade and it did not need much imagination on his part to realize what they were doing. There were cattle in those pens down there, long-horned steers; with men working quickly to change the brands. Were those part of the herd which had been rustled from Dodson? he wondered tightly. The feeling of bitter anger began to rise within him again and his hands tightened spasmodically on the reins in front of him. He paused for a further moment, then eased the guns slightly in their leather holsters. He went forward cautiously, eyes alert. In front of him, the trail dipped through a narrow ravine with thorn growing on either side. It looked dark and cool down there and it might offer a place from which he could observe the ranch for a while without being seen himself. Whatever happened, he did not figure on riding into Zena Clayburne's place with his eyes shut. Everything now depended on the few of her hired killers who could recognize him not being on the ranch. It seemed a reasonable risk for him to take. There was little doubt that most, if not all of these men, would be in town, searching for him, or riding posse with Sheriff Jason to the south of Cochita City where they had expected him to ride. But before he went down there to the ranch, he wanted to know exactly what he had set himself up against. How many men there were and the quickest way out of the place if the necessity arose and he had to get away in a hurry.

He put the horse down through the thorn thicket into the ravine. Here it was littered with debris and boulders that had been torn from the rocky walls by long ages of wind and rain and washed down to the bottom. Pacing slowly along, eyes alert for any slight movement, he reached the bottom. As he paused to slide out of the saddle, without any warning, a rope swished, fell over his shoulders pinning his arms to his sides, and he was flung violently backwards, hitting the ground with a blow that knocked all of the wind from his body.

Realizing that he had been tricked, that this was a trap, he tried to go for his guns, but the pull on the rope about his shoulders tightened suddenly as the man at the other end spotted this move on his part, and he was dragged roughly over the hard, uneven ground to the end of the narrow ravine, his body bruised and bleeding where the rocks and strands of thorn had cut into it. For a moment, he lost consciousness and when he regained his senses, his first impression was that someone was kicking him violently on the side of the head. A few seconds fled before he realized that the throbbing pain which jarred continually through his skull was a result of the blow he had received on the back of the head.

Lying on his back, with his hands and arms pinioned neatly to his sides by the lariat, he was unable to find out the full extent of any injuries he may have received. With an effort, he forced air down into his aching lungs. Every breath that he took sent a spasm of agony lancing through the muscles of his chest and burned like fire inside him. For a moment, his vision was blurred. Then it cleared as he fought to focus his gaze on what went on about him. For a moment, he could just make out the dark shapes of the men who stood around him, staring down at him against the glaring sunhaze that shone brilliantly in his eyes and seemed to burn its way through into his brain.

Then a gruff, harsh voice said thickly: 'He's coming round. Better take his guns, Chuck. He still looks mighty dangerous to me.'

Burt felt someone tug the Colts from their holsters, then a boot lashed out and kicked him viciously on the shin. 'That's just a taste o' what happens to trespassers on this spread,' growled another voice, nearer at hand. Bart forced his eyes to open and stay open and found himself staring up into a bearded face which was thrust to within a couple of inches of his own. 'Now I reckon you'd better tell us who you are, and what you're doing here.'

He licked his lips slowly. 'The name's Trant,' he said quickly. He forced a whining note into his voice. 'Just why did you fellas jump me like that? I came here peaceable like. No call for this.'

A guffaw of hard, cruel laughter greeted his words. The man leaned back then got to his feet. 'D'yuh know who's spread this is, mister?' he snarled.

Bart swallowed. 'Sure, they told me back in town that it

belonged to Miss Clayburne and that she might be able to offer me a job.'

There was a pause. Out of the corner of his eye, Bart saw the men glance at each other, then the tall, bearded man who seemed to be the leader of the small group said thickly: 'Reckon we ought to take him along with us and let Miss Clayburne deal with him, fellas. He said he wants to meet her.' He bent and a moment later, the rope around Bart's shoulders was slackened. He flexed the muscles of his arms slowly to relieve the soreness. But the relief from the stiffness was short-lived. The bearded man motioned one of the others forward and a moment later, Bart climbed into the saddle as the man gestured him up, and then his wrists were tied together behind his back.

'All right. Move,' ordered the leader roughly. He flicked the end of the lariat at the rump of Bart's horse and laughed harshly as it bounded forward, almost unseating him. Grimly, he was forced to hold on with his legs and thighs while the raucous laughs of the men sounded behind him as they urged on their own mounts. Tight-lipped, Bart swayed in the saddle, fighting to keep his balance. The sorrel bucked and plunged under him. Down the slope they raced with the yelling cowboys close beside him. Still weak from the bruising he had received, it was a miracle that he managed to hang on until they reached the wide courtyard which fronted the ranch.

For a moment, Bart hung in the saddle. The cord which bound his wrists had cut deeply into his flesh.

'Git down,' muttered one of the men, sliding from the saddle and walking forward. 'We'll see what Miss Clayburne figures we ought to do with yuh.'

Bart teetered for a moment as his feet touched the ground, but grimly, he held himself upright. There was still one chance for him. These men had not yet discovered the slim-bladed knife strapped to his wrist and so long as he had that there was still a slender chance.

Blinking against the strong sunlight, he peered about him. The stockade he had noticed from the hill lay to his right, less than thirty yards away and there seemed little doubt now that these were part of the herd which had been stolen at the river crossing. He pulled his lips tightly together for a moment, tried the cords which bound his wrists experimentally. But whoever had tied them had known his job and it was impossible for him to budge them. All that he succeeded in doing was to make the cord bite more deeply into his wrists. He forced himself to relax.

One of the men came forward and thrust him across the courtyard to the small corral which adjoined the stockade. It was then that Bart noticed, for the first time, the horse which raced around the corral and the tall, raven-haired woman who stood in the centre with the long whip in her right hand. He could not see her features as she stood there with her back to him, but there was something about her which made him know instantly that this was Zena Clayburne.

The stallion galloped around the corral, occasionally throwing its forelegs high into the air as the whip lashed it fiercely. For a long moment, Bart held his breath. In spite of his natural anger at seeing a good piece of horseflesh handled in this cruel manner, he felt a grudging admiration for the way in which the woman handled the creature, for the utter lack of fear which she displayed by even going into that corral with such an animal. Even he could see that it was a bad-tempered brute and needed only the slightest provocation to turn on her, once she showed any fear, or as soon as that whip stopped flicking out at it, goading it forward.

Finally, the woman seemed to tire of the sport, for she turned abruptly, and walked for the edge of the corral. The man thrust Bart forward. At the movement, Zena Clayburne looked round, came through the gate and closed it behind her. Then she came up to them and regarded Bart unwinkingly, a challenge in her level gaze.

'We caught this fella snooping around in the copse back

67

yonder, Miss Zena,' said the bearded man harshly, 'Thought you might like to take a look at him before deciding what do do. Could be that he's the law, though he don't act like it. Seems scared to me, in spite of his size.' There was a faint note of scorn in the gruff voice. It was the reaction that Bart had wanted and he felt an inward satisfaction.

'Well'?' Zena Clayburne's brows went up expressively. She still held the whip coiled in her hands and ran it through her fingers meaningly as she watched him closely. 'What were you doing riding on my land?'

'I rode in through town yesterday,' he said quietly. 'I figured I might get a job on one of the spreads around here, but when I asked at those to the south, seemed they were so small that they didn't need help of any kind. They told me in town that you were the biggest landowner in these parts, so I came riding out here looking for work. I can do most anything around a ranch. Ride herd, mend fences.'

She eyed him appraisingly. There was a faint gleam of cunning at the back of the dark eyes and a hard expression on her regular features. Zena Clayburne was a very striking woman, thought Bart inwardly, as he watched her from beneath lowered lids. Tall, about thirty-five years of age, her dark looks spoke of a Spanish or Mexican ancestry. She could have been classed as beautiful had it not been for the hard, determined set of the full lips and the cruel look in her eyes. He did not doubt, now that he had met her face to face, that she was the kind of woman who could build an empire out here, either by fair deeds or foul. She would allow nothing to stand in her way. He had seen the way she had handled that horse in the corral, and he knew that she would have the same kind of contemptuous disdain for a man.

'You say you rode through Cochita City yesterday.' There was a note of interest in her tone, an interrogatory note. 'Did you happen to hear of a man they brought in from one of the ranches to the south? A man who had been with that outlaw party that raided a herding party some days ago.'

Bart nodded slowly. 'Did hear about him,' he admitted. 'Heard that he was in the jailhouse and they were figuring on hanging him before sundown. Some of the folk there were a mite sore at the sheriff for keeping him locked away in the jail. Seems they thought he ought to hang first and they'd ask any necessary questions afterwards. There was a talk of a lynching party after sundown.'

Zena Clayburne's smile was not a pleasant thing and Bart felt his skin tingle and the small hairs on the back of his neck began to ruffle uncomfortably.

'It seems that they didn't succeed,' she retorted thinly. 'I wanted that man killed because he was a menace as far as I'm concerned. Once the rest of my men ride in from town, I'll get the full story. It seems that I'm surrounded by men who can't obey orders, even when they're simple ones like seeing to it that a man dies.' She tapped the stock of the whip against the palm of her open hand. There was a speculative look in her eyes.

'You could be telling me the truth about wanting a job here,' she said musingly. 'But on the other hand, you might be the law, as Clem seems to think. And in my position here, with so much at stake, I can't afford to take any chances.'

'Chances?' Bart looked at her in surprise. 'I'm afraid I don't understand, ma'am. All I want is a job. If there ain't any going, I'll ride on and try my luck further west.'

Zena Clayburne smiled again, turned to the burly man who stood beside her in respectful silence. 'Do you think that he's telling the truth, Clem? It might pay us to make sure.'

The other nodded and there was a look of fierce expectation at the back of the deep-set eyes. 'Could be that he's the law,' repeated the other slowly. 'It might be that word of our rustling has got back east and they've sent someone out to investigate. Won't be too difficult to make him talk.'

'And how can you be sure that he'll tell the truth?'

The man's dark face was alive with savage triumph, 'He'll tell the truth, Miss Zena. I promise you that.'

The woman paused, then turned to face Bart. 'Seems like my foreman has a point there,' she said smoothly. 'Something else too. You could even be the man we're looking for, though I doubt it. Not even he would have such a low regard for his life as to ride in here like this.'

'Now listen, ma'am,' began Bart. He stepped forward, then reeled back as a tightly-bunched fist caught him flush on the side of the face. Hitting the side of the corral he went down on to his knees, struggled upright, feeling the blood trickling from his mouth and down the side of his bruised face. He shook his head in an effort to clear it.

In spite of the blow, be persisted. 'I'm a peace-loving man,' he went on thickly. 'I didn't ride here looking for trouble. I don't know what all this is about, but I want no part of it.'

'You rode in carrying two guns,' said Clem, nodding slowly. 'And from the way you rode down into that ravine, I'd say you were trying to spy out the lie of the land for some reason known only to yourself. There's a lot that you ain't told us, stranger, and I figger that the sooner we know the truth, the better.'

He tried to sway his head sideways as he sensed the fist coming in again, but it caught him on the cheek, throwing him to one side. His head rang with the shuddering impact. His bruised body protested. Zena Clayburne made no move to stop the unequal contest, but merely stood watching with a faintly amused expression on her features.

'You won't get away with this,' he mumbled through swollen lips. 'Once the sheriff hears about this, he'll—'

'Sheriff Jason may be only too pleased to hear of what has happened,' said the woman softly. Then her voice hardened abruptly. 'But we've wasted enough time. Clem – tie him up and make him talk. I want to know who he really is and what he's doing here. And hurry. If he is the law, there may be more of them out there somewhere and we'll have to strike first.' The ruthless quality in her voice made Bart shiver. He knew that these people would not kill him out of hand yet –

not until they had learned everything they wanted from him. And there was still the knife strapped to his wrist.

Roughly, the bearded man caught him by the arm, forced him back across the courtyard. Bart had no illusions as to what the others intended to do with him. The suspicion had been planted in the woman's mind and even if there was only the faintest chance that he was part of the law, she had to make certain that he was dead; otherwise her future here was worth nothing. At the far side of the courtyard, near the house, a stout pole had been driven into the ground. Bart guessed that it had been once used to tether a horse to, until the corral had been built and it had been no longer necessary to exercise and break the wild horses in the courtyard itself. Now they had found another use for it. Releasing his hands, two men gripped a wrist apiece and forced his arms back, while they tied him securely to the post. The position was intensely painful and he guessed that these men had learned this old trick from the Indians at some time or other. It was impossible for him to lower his head and he was forced to stare up into the blue-white mirror of the sky where the sun still burned in a fiery disc. The harsh, brilliant light forced itself past his eyelids, even when he tried to screw up his eyes, burning into his brain.

Clem came forward, thrust his face up close to Bart's. 'You still say that you were just riding out here looking for a job, mister?' he demanded harshly.

Rigidly, Bart tried to nod his head. Deliberately, he held his tongue.

Without another word, the big man turned on his heel and walked away from Bart, pausing about twenty paces away. He said something to the woman, but it was impossible for Bart to make out the words. Then he turned, pulled something from his belt and balanced it carefully in the palm of his right hand. The sunlight glinted brilliantly on the broad blade of the heavy-hafted knife.

Without warning, his right arm swung up and then

71

forward, flashing through the sunlight, embedding itself in the wood of the post with a faint thud. Bart felt the sharp sting, followed by a trickle of warm blood down the side of his face and realized that the keen edge of the blade had missed his skull by a hair's breadth and had nicked the lobe of his ear. He held himself stiffly upright, allowing the air to flow out of his lungs in a slow, steady exhalation.

'Still insist that you came here only looking for a job, stranger?' The woman's voice broke in on the thoughts that were racing through Bart's mind. 'Better talk before Clem here loses his patience and decides to put one of his knives between your eyes.'

'I don't know what it is you want me to say,' he gritted, tugging on the cord which held him. 'I don't know anything about the law, or this man you talk of, that they were supposed to hang in town.'

'Perhaps you don't, but this ought to loosen your tongue, just in case you think you can lie to me.' The hardness was still there in Zena Clayburne's voice and he knew that he could expect no mercy from her. A medley of mocking yells came from the men who crowded close to the corral rails, watching the scene which was being enacted in front of them. This was something to relieve the monotony of cow-punching and to these hardened gunslingers, this provided the entertainment they craved.

Clem, his body bent slightly forward, plucked a second knife from his belt and stood for a moment, turning it over and over in his hands. Bart could feel the sweat beginning to form on his forehead, to trickle down his face, into his eyes, half blinding him. He lifted his right arm, stood for a moment with his eyes on the woman. For an instant, she paused, then gave a quick nod. The arm flashed forward and downward and Bart felt the wind of the blade as it whipped past his cheek and thudded into the tough wood. With unwinking eyes, he pulled his head up as far as possible and forced himself to stare across the intervening space at his tormentor. That

72

second knife had missed him by less than half an inch. The next time, if Zena Clayburne decided that he knew nothing, the third weapon would kill him. They could not afford to let him go now, he realized. They had to kill him. But somehow, he did not think that they would do it this way, in full view of all the men on the ranch. There were bound to be a few of them – not many perhaps – who were not crooked cowpunchers and gunslammers, and Gena Clayburne would not want these men to know that she had allowed a man to be murdered in cold blood. Her position here was powerful, but there might still be a strong faction in the town who could turn against her and at the moment, he doubted if she would be willing to take the risk of having them band together and rise against her. He recalled the way in which the decent citizens of Cochita City had wanted to lynch him, believing the lies that had been spread about him, that he was one of the outlaws captured by the sheriff and his posse. Believing that, it did not require too much imagination to understand how they might feel if they had positive proof of Zena Clayburne's complicity with these rustlers and killers.

No, when she decided that she knew all there was to know about him, she would make certain that he was killed – but it would have to be done discreetly, by someone she could trust and well away from the ranch. This was what he was gambling on, this was the only thing which might save him now that he had ridden into the enemy camp.

'Still not talking, mister?' For a moment, Bart thought that there would be a third knife coming to part his hair, but the blow which came was not from a sharp-bladed knife, rather it was a streak of pain that curled about his chest, cutting through the cloth of his shirt. He had forgotten about the whip which the woman still held in her hand. Now it was lashing fiercely at him, cutting into his skin. He gritted his teeth tightly. Suddenly, there seemed no chance of escape from this lashing, flicking length of torment that seemed to come at his body from all sides.

73

Like a dazed man, the cowboy hung against the cords that bound him to the post. This savagery of Zena Clayburne's amounted almost to madness, his tired brain told him. There was fear too at the back of it. Fear that the law had now finally caught up with her, threatening the whole edifice that she had built here in this frontier territory, so that she could no longer be the mistress of these lands, this cattle empire that she had built up by going directly against the law.

Wooden-faced, he pulled himself upright, staring solidly at the woman who stood in front of him with death written plainly in her dark eyes. His head still throbbed from the rough treatment he had received when these men had captured him and his arm muscles ached under the strain to which they were being subjected. But he knew that he must show no sign of weakness here, that was exactly what these fiends were looking for.

The whip struck him again across the body sending an agony of pain lancing through him. Then the woman paused. 'Perhaps he is telling the truth,' she said harshly to the man standing beside her. She walked forward until she stood directly in front of him. Her mouth was tight, but a sudden smile showed on her lips. 'If you're a wise man, you'll forget what happened,' she said softly, but there was an underlying note of menace in her voice. 'We don't like snoopers or trespassers here and we have our own ways of dealing with them.'

'You're a fool if you think you can get away with this,' he rasped, forcing the words out through swollen lips. Out of the corner of his eye, he saw the tall, black-bearded man step forward suddenly, his bunched fist drawn back. But the woman put out a slim hand and touched his arm.

'I'll handle this, Clem,' she said softly. 'I'm sure our friend here will realize that we had to do this. Besides,' she paused and turned to Bart, eyeing him speculatively, 'if you ride into town and try to tell this to the sheriff, you'll find that you'll get no help from him. I'll swear out a warrant that you were caught on my spread trying to rustle my cattle. They're look-

74

ing for cattle rustlers in Cochita City now and you'll find that it'll be my word against yours. I think you'll find that the sheriff will be more willing to believe me than you.'

She nodded towards Clem, 'Cut him loose. See that he's given something to eat and then ride with him to the edge of the spread. Make sure that he doesn't come back.'

From beneath lowered lids, Bart noticed the swift glance that passed between the woman and the burly killer and knew what lay behind those words. He was to be taken to some remote part of the spread and then the showdown would come.

'You'd better take Jake with you, in case he decides to make trouble,' added Zena Clayburne meaningly. 'He looks like a dangerous man to me.'

'He won't make any trouble,' muttered the other fiercely. He fingered the two knives which still rested in his belt.

'Perhaps not. But I still want Jake to ride with you.'

The other shrugged, then stepped forward, plucked one of the knives from the post close to Bart's face and went behind him, slicing through the ropes around his wrists. They loosened and then fell away. Bart lowered his arms slightly to relieve the numbing ache that spread up from his wrists. He looked at the woman.

'I don't know what it is you're trying to do here,' he said thinly. 'But I don't think I'd take a job here even if you offered me one.' His words were a deliberate insult. He saw her flush and the hand that gripped the whip tightened suddenly. For a moment, she seemed on the point of slashing him across the face with it, then she relaxed. 'Don't try to provoke me any further,' she snapped, 'or I might reconsider my offer to let you ride off my land. Take your horse and get out. If I see you here again, I'll kill you.'

'Don't worry,' he said, thickly. 'I won't be coming back.'

Seated in the saddle, Bart stared straight ahead of him for a moment. His body seemed to have been battered all over and

75

every movement sent a fresh stab of pain through him. The two men who rode, one on either side of him, were silent, faces grim. He said quietly: 'Just what are you men figgering to do when we get to the edge of the spread. Shoot me in the back and spread it around that I was shot trying to run away? They'd probably believe that in the sheriff's office in Cochita City, but there'll always be some folk who'll ask questions.'

'Shut up,' growled Clem harshly. 'You talk too much.'

Bart grinned mirthlessly, twisting in his saddle to watch him. 'You ain't foolin' me none,' he said tonelessly. 'Do you think I was taken in by all that talk back there at the ranch. I know what your orders really are. You're to see that I don't get back to town and talk about what happened here this afternoon. You're afraid, just as Zena Clayburne is afraid, that I know too much, that I saw that herd you were busy altering the brands on in your stockade.'

Clem swung sharply in the saddle and his hand hovered dangerously close to the gun at his waist. 'I warned you,' he gritted harshly. 'I ain't telling you again. Keep yore mouth shut and you'll stay in one piece. We've been told to ride you off this spread, and that's what we're aiming to do. If you try to make things tough for us, then I ain't going to answer to what we might have to do.'

Bart sat silent, thinking his turbulent thoughts, trying to fill in some of the many empty spaces in his knowledge. He had not expected two men to ride with him like this and that complicated matters more than he had anticipated. He had reckoned on only having to deal with one man. The knife would be quick and sure and then he intended making it back into town, riding in after dark, and looking out this editor who had been a good friend of the late sheriff's. Perhaps the other would not be able to help him as much as he wanted, but it would be a start. There were close on ten thousand head of cattle on the Clayburne range and he intended to save these for the small ranchers from whom they had been rustled, even if it meant that he would have to fight

Zena Clayburne and her hired killers alone and unaided. But there was just the chance that this man in Cochita City might be the man to help him swing a few of the other people on to his side. In his mind's eye, looking ahead, he could foresee a time when open range war broke out in this territory, because Zena Clayburne, vicious and ambitious, would never go down without a tremendous struggle. But before any of this could happen, he had to deal with these two men. He threw quick, wary glances at each of them in turn, trying to decide which represented the most danger to him. Tall and hard, the man called Clem sat easily in the saddle, the beard jutting forward in an aggressive line as he stared straight ahead of him from beneath shaggy black brows. There was no doubt that the other was searching the ground ahead, looking for the best place to finish off Bart Shannon. The other man, Jake, was smaller with a thin, hungry look and close-set eyes. A cunning man, possibly quick with a gun, decided Bart. He seemed suspicious and his eyes were never still, flashing from side to side, his hand very close to the butt of the gun slung low at his waist.

This was the more dangerous man of the two, Bart decided, a moment later. He would move with the speed of a striking rattler for that gun and he wouldn't hesitate to shoot to kill, whereas Clem seemed to have made up his mind that Bart was going to die slowly.

Bart moved very gently in his saddle, easing his left hand forward until his finger and thumb rested very close to the knife just hidden under his sleeve. Sitting deep to ease his back, he threw a swift glance at the trail in front of them. It wound around the collar of a low hill and then down the other side, to a position where it ran along the uppermost edge of a deep crevasse filled with thorn and cottonwood. Bart's gaze rested there for a long moment, down there a man's body could remain hidden for a long while, until his face and name had been forgotten. He knew with a sudden certainty that it was here that these men intended to kill him.

His hands flexed for a moment on the pommel of the saddle.

They rode closer to the place and Bart felt his whole body tense. In front of him, Jake reined his mount, sat for a long moment staring down into the riot of trees and bushes below them, some twenty feet down the edge of the trail. There was a speculative look in his deep-set eyes and a faint, sneering grin on his face. He looked back at Clem, twisting round in the saddle. 'Well, well, it would be a pity if a man were to drop down there and break his neck on the rocks,' he drawled. 'Especially after we'd taken so much trouble to bring him all the way out here. Still, accidents will happen, I guess.'

'So you do intend to kill me,' said Bart thinly.

The other sneered. 'Seems the only choice we have, mister. You might be who you say you are, but on the other hand, you could be the law. We had a couple of lawmen snooping around here a while ago. They tried to find out about the herd back there and we had to stop them from getting back east with the information they got.'

'How long do you figure you can keep a thing like this from getting out into the open?' demanded Bart. He kept his eyes on the other, his gaze locking with his.

'Long enough,' Jake laughed scornfully. 'Reckon this is where you take a header into Hell, cowboy. Pity you had to come snooping around here. Otherwise you might've stayed alive.' He lowered his hand to the gun in its holster, his fingers closed tightly around it as he jerked it free. He took his time, anticipating no trouble from the unarmed man who sat the saddle in front of him. The thin lips drew back in a sneer of evil triumph. 'This is where you get it, cowboy,' he said jubilantly.

From the corner of his eye, Bart noticed that the big man was sitting easily in the saddle, his hands resting in front of him, obviously enjoying what was happening, but not wishing to take any part in it himself. He was there merely to see that everything went according to plan and that Bart Shannon did not remain alive to cause them any further trouble.

78

Jake lifted the long barrel in a slow, sweeping draw to bring it in line with Bart's chest. It was almost on its target, with the outlaw's finger showing white on the trigger, when Bart's left hand moved in a sudden, totally unexpected blur of speed. For a split second, the knife was balanced on the palm of his hand. Then it was flashing through the air swifter than the eye could see. The thin faced man stiffened abruptly in his saddle, the gun toppling out of his nerveless fingers as the blade buried itself up to the haft in his throat. There was a look of frozen amazement on his dark, saturnine features as he remained upright in the saddle for a brief instant, then toppled sideways with a faint, rattling cry, pitching over the side of the trail, his body turning over and over before it crashed into the branches of the trees down below. For one staggering moment, there was absolute silence. Even as Bart turned his head to face the other, Clem tried to go for his guns. Only split second timing saved Bart's life then. There was no time to try to ride out before the other plucked the guns from their holsters. He had already made up his mind what he intended to do even before he had thrown that knife. Swiftly, he hurled himself to one side, arms outstretched, catching the other around the middle and hurling him out of the saddle. Both men hit the ground with a bone-shaking impact. Gasping breath, Bart threw himself on top of the other, slammed with his bunched fist at the bearded face beneath him. He felt his knuckles rasp along the other's jaw, tearing the skin. Clem gave a harsh bellow of rage that sounded like a bull, and heaved upwards with all of his strength, no longer going for his guns, but thrusting up with his great hands, trying to fasten them around Bart's throat, the fingers flexed. Swiftly, Bart heaved his head back, striving to keep it out of range of those terrible hands, knowing that if the other managed to get a grip on him, nothing but death would make him release it.

Savagely, he clubbed downward again with his fist. But Clem had turned his head on one side and the blow glanced

79

harmlessly off the side of his skull. Madly, he tried to hold on as the other kicked upward, but the man's strength was phenomenal. Thrown on to his back, Bart rolled swiftly to one side as the other came at him, kicking savagely. The rowel of a spur scraped along Bart's arm, ripping through the cloth of his sleeve, drawing blood. There was just time to roll away again, to scramble to his feet before the other came charging in, bellowing loudly, angrily. Arms wide, Clem bored in, kicking with his feet, so that the spurts of dust rose into Bart's eyes, half-blinding him. Jabbing with his left fist, he caught the other flush on the nose, felt the cartilage smash under the blow, saw the spurt of blood. But the other still came on with a howl of rage, ignoring the blow, brushing aside Bart's other hand as he hammered at the outlaw's head. Thrusting forward with all of his tremendous weight, the other caught Bart about the middle, threw him back on to the ground. He hit hard on his shoulder blades, felt the sharp-edged pieces of rock bore into his back. He was now almost on the edge of the trail. Below him lay the thirty foot drop down which the body of Jake had plunged but a few moments earlier with Bart's knife in his throat.

Clem seemed to be putting every ounce of strength he had into sliding Bart's body over the edge. He leaned back and caught him around the knees, thrusting him along the ground. Savagely, desperately, Bart kicked out, felt his toe strike the other full in the chest. Clem staggered back, all of the air driven out of his body by the force of the blow. Gasping for breath, his mouth hanging slackly open, his eyes staring, he stood upright for a moment, fighting for balance.

Bart staggered up. His body felt as if it had been hit by a mule, but he knew that he had to fight this man, because nothing less than his own death would satisfy Clem now. He was determined to kill him with his bare hands. Clem was scrambling up off his knees as Bart moved forward, judging his swing, trying to keep his eyes focused on the gunslinger. Savagely, he hit the other again, this time on the side of the head as Clem charged. His fist struck rock-hard bone and pain jarred along his arm. For a moment, it felt as if he had broken his hand on the other's skull. But the blow had jolted the killer, for he stepped back and blinked his eyes several times. There was blood running from the side of his mouth, dribbling down his bearded chin. Then the gunslammer's big fist seemed to capsize Bart's chest as it connected. All of the air seemed to have been pushed out of his lungs and his ribs seemed to have been caved in by the tremendous force of that solid blow. He gave ground, skipping to one side as the other attempted to rush him again, to sweep him off his feet and knock him down into the bushes below after Jake.

Blinking to clear his vision and the ringing in his head, Bart side-stepped, gave ground again, sucking air back into his chest. He had the odd feeling that at any moment now, the other would realize that there was a quicker and easier way of getting rid of him, and his hand would drop to the guns at his waist and a bullet would finish the task for him.

CHAPTER V

THE LONE STRANGER

There was still a ringing in Bart's head as he struggled to get to his feet but he could feel some of the strength surging back into his arms and legs and he seemed to have got his second wind. Slowly, his vision was clearing. He was still poised very close to the edge of the trail where it fell abruptly away to the gorge below but now he saw that most of his earlier blows had had their effect on the bigger man. The gunslinger had almost killed him with those first kicks and wild, vicious swings, but he was gasping now like a fish out of water, trying desperately to draw air down into that cavernous, heaving chest.

The outlaw's eyes, narrowed a little now that Bart had succeeded in manoeuvring him so that the sun was glaring directly into his face, shone with the killing fever as he came crowding in after Bart. His fingers were no longer bunched into tight fists, but spread wide, clawed, ready to rip and tear and squeeze.

Clem wouldn't use his guns now to kill him, Bart thought fiercely, with a sudden certainty. He wanted, more than anything else, to kill him with his bare hands, to feel those thick fingers squeeze the life out of him, for only thus could he be certain of satisfying the blood lust that raged strongly within him. Bart dug in his heels and waited for the other to come to him, ready for any move the outlaw might make. For some strange reason, his mind seemed to be cool and unnaturally clear now, with all of that mental fog washed away by the knowledge that he had to kill this man or be killed himself. Hate boiled up inside him, tightening the muscles of his stomach and chest as he watched the other move slowly forward, arms swinging loosely, his whole body poised. There was hate for these men who had killed his own companions, shot them down in cold blood on the banks of that wide river and then ridden off with their herd, hate against Zena Clayburne who had so calmly arranged for him to die out here at the hands of these two hired killers. Well, he thought tightly, she was going to discover it wasn't as easy as that to get rid of him.

It was this boiling hatred which gave him the edge of the other, bigger man. Rage blinded the outlaw's movements, made him over-confident. Perhaps it was the knowledge that Bart still had his back to that thirty-foot drop into death which made him forget all caution. He paused for a brief moment, then rushed in fast, without any warning, arms reaching forward, hoping to bear his opponent back over the edge by sheer weight and strength.

Bart waited for him calmly. His mind was razor-sharp now. Stepping inside the circle of the other's arms, he swung hard, two short, shaking jabs to the man's face. Clem grunted, reeled back, arms still wide. Without pause, Bart followed up his advantage. Two more thrusting, heeling slashes with the sides of his hands against the other's bull-like neck, just behind the ears; vicious, chopping blows that stopped the other in his tracks. For a moment, Clem stood there, fighting to clear his head, swaying slightly, refusing to go down under blows that had been delivered with sufficient speed and strength to render any normal man unconscious.

Shaking his head, he staggered back, then lumbered forward once more, driven on by instinct, desperately trying to get his arms around his opponent; now a shadow that danced and swayed tantalizingly in front of him, enticing him further forward, towards that precipitous drop which would lead a man into eternity. Dropping his right shoulder, Bart drove it forward with the speed of a battering ram full into the other's stomach. Grunting once more, Clem backed up, eyes glazing. Then, with a desperate, heaving surge of strength, dragged up from the dregs of his endurance, he swung forward, taking Bart completely by surprise. His huge arms licked out, clamped a tight hold around Bart's body and began to squeeze inexorably, pulling tighter about his waist, bending him back as he leaned the whole of his tremendous weight upon the other. Gasping for breath, Bart struggled to free his arms, pinioned to his sides by the bear hug. But it was impossible to move them. This was a move that the other evidently knew to perfection. Slowly, inexorably, he began to increase the pressure, his face thrust close into Bart's, lips drawn back into an animal-like sneer of triumph.

Bart felt himself being lifted off his feet, pulled upwards as the other tried to move forward with him, right to the very edge of the trail. There was no doubting the other's intentions now. He intended to squeeze him into submission and then drop his limp body over the side. Savagely, Bart butted the other in the face with the top of his skull, but this only served to make the other increase the dizzying pressure still further until it seemed impossible that Bart could hold out any longer. There was a limit to the bending that a human spine could take and he knew with a sick certainty that he was almost at the limit of his. There was a roaring in his ears and a savage throbbing at the back of his temples as the blood pounded incessantly through his veins. His eyes seemed to be on the point of bursting out of their sockets.

Again and again, he pounded at the other's face, then

suddenly switched his attack and brought his upright knee into the pit of the other's stomach. The move took the gunslinger completely by surprise. With a bellow of savage pain, the hold around Bart's waist slackened, not completely, but enough for him to be able to suck some air down into his heaving lungs, and to get both arms free of the hold.

Sobbing for breath, he paused for a moment as everything threatened to spin around him. Clem had been hurt, but he was still the stronger of the two. A second later, Bart smashed two quick, brutal blows with the flat of his hand at the other's neck. Roaring angrily, the other tried to swing him backward, off his feet, but this was a move for which Bart had been prepared. Before the other could regain his balance, he had hooked his foot behind the gunman's shin and heaved with all of his strength. The arms around his body fell away as the other tried desperately to remain upright. Too late, he saw that they were far closer to the edge of the trail than he had imagined. For a moment, he seemed to sway outward from the rocky lip of the trail, arms flailing ineffectually as he strove wildly to pull himself upright. Then the edge crumbled away from him, a shower of small stones falllng down the slope as he plunged over the edge. Gasping for air, Bart stood and watched the other's body turning over slowly as it fell. There was only one single wild scream from the other; a weird and terrible sound that floated up from the depths a few moments before Clem's body hit the topmost branches of the trees and crashed out of sight.

Bart took his time. He had a little trouble standing and when he moved his legs, they felt as though they had been battered to a jelly by the punishment they had taken. He stepped away from the lip of the ravine and staggered over to where the three horses stood waiting. He was still without any weapons. Jake had gone down to his death with his knife still in his throat and Clem's guns had still been pouched when he had died. He had been so sure of victory that he had never tried to go for them and do things the easy way. Now he had paid for that with his life.

Bart sat down heavily by the side of the trail and threw an anxious look behind him. From there he could see most of the trail where it ran back towards the Clayburne ranch, but there was no sign that Zena Clayburne had sent anyone else out along the trail, just to make certain that this time, he was finished for good. Whether or not she had believed him to be the man she wanted dead, he did not know. By now, she would be feeling certain that if he was, then he would be dead and no longer any menace to her. And if not, then there would always be the chance that Sheriff Jason might justify his existence and bring him in. Either way, she would be feeling quite pleased with herself, he thought, smiling grimly to himself.

How long he sat there, waiting for life to come back into his bruised body, he did not know. He had no sense of time and he didn't know whether he rested by the side of the trail for one minute or twenty. The brutal beating that he had taken at the hands of the gunman had left him numb in feelings as well as in body. A little of the hatred and anger that had triggered his fists and given him the necessary strength to kill both of those two outlaws was beginning to fade a little, to sink away into the background of his mind. It would never go away entirely until he had finished what he had sworn to do. See to it that every man in that rustling party and the woman behind it, were dead or in jail. And to do that it was essential that he should find someone to help him. He could not hope to destroy them all single-handed and even the Guthries would not be enough to back him up if it came to a real showdown.

He felt a faint twinge of righteous anger, this time against the ordinary, decent citizens of Cochita City and the small ranchers of the surrounding territory. Surely they ought to have realized by now that they had it in their power to rid the country of this menace, this evil scourge which had descended upon them like a swarm of locusts. If they persisted in allowing Zena Clayburne to take them over and destroy them one at a time, it would not be long before they were all killed or thrown off their lands. After a while, he got to his feet. His brain moved slow, sluggish, as though unable to follow the trail of thought that he wanted it to follow. There was just the possibility that this man, Ben Wheeler, who seemed to be the only person in Cochita City that he could trust with his identity, might be able to help him. Everything would depend on how far the other was willing to go for the real truth about Zena Clayburne to come out into the open. If he so much as printed a word of that, together with any real evidence that he might be able to give him, it would mean the other's life, if Zena ever got wind of it. A man like Ben Wheeler, if he started printing the truth, would be a very dangerous man as far as she was concerned. Almost as dangerous as Bart Shannon.

Throwing one last glance back along the trail, he climbed up into the saddle, roped in the other two horses and rode them with him as he headed for the boundary of the spread. He did not want two riderless horses showing up at the Clayburne ranch until he was good and ready. When her two killers failed to show up that night, Zena Clayburne would figure that something had gone wrong with her plan and she would send out men to look for them. The longer it took these men to find those bodies, the more chance he had of getting into town unseen and talking with this editor.

He let the two horses go once he had cleared the Clayburne spread and watched for a moment as they galloped off to the east. They would not be easy to find out here, he told himself as he turned his own mount and set its face for Cochita City. Already, the sun was beginning to lower towards the western horizon and there were long shadows everywhere. As he rode, he kept his eyes continually on the move, alert for any sign of pursuit. He told himself that this was not the only

87

direction from which danger might come. Sheriff Jason and his posse were out somewhere in the territory trying to ride him down, thinking that he had gone to earth further to the south. But if they failed to find him there, they might ride back to report to Zena Clayburne that night and if he was not watchful he might ride straight into them. He had gone through too much to be picked up like that.

He took the high trail that wound among the bluffs to the north-east, skirting the main trail, knowing that the chance of discovery was greater down there. Once, as he paused among the rocks, he heard the distant thunder of horses moving across the plain and a few moments later, caught sight of the band of men, riding hard, pushing their mounts to the utmost. They were heading up from the south, from beyond the town, but from that distance, it was impossible for him to determine whether it was the sheriff and the posse or not. Whoever it was, they were in a goddurned hurry, he told himself and they seemed to be taking the trail for the Clayburne place.

Edging around the town, he came in from the west, keeping to the deeper shadows as much as he could. The town was still alive. Music came from the saloons along the main street and there were lights in most of the buildings. He slid from the saddle and stood on the boardwalk at the intersection of the main street and one of the smaller, darker alleys which led off from it. When he had ridden into town a couple of days earlier, he had made a mental note of where most of the places were and had spotted the small, poky little place where Ben Wheeler brought out the only newspaper in the place. It was an unpretentious building, needed a fresh coat of paint and looked as though it had been neglected for many years. The life of a small town editor in the frontier was never an easy one. He always seemed to make more enemies than friends and he had to be an honest man of integrity. Such men did not often live long out here unless they printed exactly what they were told to print. Ben Wheeler had already received one warning of what might happen to him if he went against Zena Clayburne. Since then, apparently, he had steered clear of mentioning her. Perhaps he would not want to rake up anything else and run the risk of being shot and possibly killed outright.

He slipped into the small shop through the back way, eyes narrowed. The door at the rear of the building was open and he went inside, closing it carefully behind him, listening intently for any sound. There was always the strong possibility that Ben Wheeler might be expecting someone to come for him like this and he would be a man to shoot first and ask questions later. There was a risk here, but it was one he had to take.

Slowly, he worked his way along a narrow passage which led through the building to the front of the shop where the printing press would be set up. He tried to rack his brains as he moved forward on noiseless feet, trying to recall whether or not Tess had mentioned whether Ben Wheeler stayed on the premises after dark, or whether he lived somewhere else in town. There was also the chance that he might be over in one of the saloons, and the place would be empty. The door at the end of the passage was closed. For a long moment, he paused behind it, trying to make out any sound in the room beyond. At first, he could hear nothing and he was on the point of turning the handle of the door, thrusting it open, and walking through, when he heard the sound. It was an oddly metallic noise that he could not place, but it told him that the building was not empty and that the chances were that Ben Wheeler was through there.

He hesitated for only another second, then twisted the handle sharply and went through. Bart had a glimpse of a tall, white-haired man bent over the printing press in the middle of the room as he shut the door behind him. Then the other whirled swiftly, stood upright and stared across the room at him. Almost before Bart could move, the other's right hand went down and then came up again, holding a heavy, long-barrelled weapon in it, trained on Bart's chest.

'Now you just stand right there.' The man's voice was steady and harsh. 'If you make one funny move, I'll kill you.'

'Listen, Wheeler,' said Bart quickly. 'I came here to talk to you. This is very important and—'

The other laughed harshly, a short bark of sound. He jerked the gun up again meaningly as Bart walked forward a couple of paces. 'Just stay there.' There was no doubting the resolution in the old man's voice. 'I know who you are, and why you came here, sneaking in through the back, hoping to take me by surprise and shoot me down.'

'You've got me all wrong, Wheeler,' said Bart harshly. He walked forward very slowly, keeping his hands in sight all of the time. He knew that the other, in spite of his outward look of calm, was jumpy, and a frightened man needed little excuse to pull a trigger. 'I came here because a friend of yours told me you were the only man in the town I could trust to help me against Zena Clayburne.'

The other eyed him suspiciously, but the gun did not waver by so much as a single inch, remaining on his chest. 'A friend of mine, you say. I ain't got many friends in Cochita City since – well, some years back anyway, so you're lying on that point, mister. Now I reckon you'd better talk and tell me just why you are here afore I decide to pull this trigger. I know Zena Clayburne's been trying to kill me for some time, only she's never been able to do it so that it looks legal. Could be that she figures she can send one of her killers to do the job for her.' The other screwed up his eyes, forehead wrinkling. 'Say, I ain't never noticed you around these parts before.' The suspicious look intensified. His thin lips tightened. 'So she reckons she'll send a stranger, a gunman out of town.'

Bart shook his head. 'I don't come from Zena Clayburne,' he said emphatically and turned his head slightly to look about him. There were stacks of paper in one corner of the room and some scattered around the printing press, with bottles of ink littering the top of the solitary desk near the window. Bart took all of this in with a single, sweeping glance, noticing also that even though the shutters had been put up across the window, there was only the flickering dim light of a hurricane lamp on the desk to illuminate the room.

'Where do you come from then, mister?' No let up of the suspicion in the old man's voice. 'Speak up and it had better be good.'

'You knew old Sheriff Keene before he was killed.'

'So I knew him. What of it?'

'Tess Guthrie also reckons that you know where there might be some evidence showing that Zena Clayburne is connected with his murder.'

'Tess?' The other came forward and peered up into Bart's face. Then he lowered the long-barrelled gun in his hand and relaxed visibly. 'You're Bart Shannon.'

'That's right, old-timer,' Bart nodded. 'You've seen Tess then?'

'Saw her this morning. She's a fine girl, but she's a mite foolish if she reckons she can stop Zena Clayburne. That woman is worse than a mountain cat. She'll stop at nothing, even murder.'

'Then you think there might be evidence that she was implicated in the sheriff's murder?'

'Sure of it,' said the other emphatically. 'But it ain't going to be easy to get it. You don't figure they keep anything like that around where anybody can lay their hands on it, do you?'

'Probably not, but if you could give me a lead as to where it was, I could see if I could get it. We need something concrete like that before we can get any of these others on to our side. As it is, they seem content to sit back and let the others be killed or run out of the territory by this woman.' He seated himself in the chair at the table and looked across at the other, then jerked a thumb in the direction of the press. 'Seems to me you were printing something there you didn't want anyone else to see. Not with those shuttered up and hardly any light in the room.'

A faint smile touched the other's lips and he nodded slowly. 'I'm an old man,' he explained, lowering himself into the other chair. 'I'm almost past fighting, and there have been many times in the past when I doubted whether there was anything left here worth fighting for. But somebody has to try to stop Zena Clayburne and those gunslingers she has on that spread. Otherwise, they'll overrun the whole territory and the place will be fit for only gunmen and the lawless breed. I fought in the early days to keep that breed out of here. I helped to turn back the cattle men when they tried to take over the town. When the range war started between them and the nesters, I tried to stop it. Then Zena Clayburne moved in and for once, there seemed to be nothing I could do. But I'm almost at the end now, and I reckoned I'd have one last, desperate fling. I was going to denounce them for the killers they are. I know what they threatened to do the last time I printed anything like this. And I don't doubt that they'll carry out their threat this time. But even if they do succeed in killing one old man, it might stir the others to take action before it's too late.'

'You'd take that risk, just to stir up these people here?' asked Bart incredulously. He began to revise his opinion of this man. There was fear in him, but something else, something high and noble that swamped out the fear. Getting to his feet, Wheeler walked over to the press, picked up one of the printed sheets which lay beside it, the ink still wet on the paper and brought it over to Bart. Thrusting it into the other's hand, he commanded sharply: 'Read it. Let me know if you think there ought to be anything else I can say about those coyotes. I don't reckon they'll let me bring out a second edition of this, and I want to be sure there's everything in it.'

Bart read through it carefully. When he had finished, he laid it down on the table and stared across at the other. 'That's dynamite,' he said softly. 'If the people here could only have proof of what you say in that, they might decide they've had enough of Zena Clayburne and her men and take the law into their own hands. But as it stands, they might not believe it.'

'You mean that they might not want to believe it,' said the other, with a ring of scorn in his voice. 'I've lived in this town for the best part of forty-seven years, almost from the day that it was brought into being. Sometimes, I feel sickened by the way the townsfolk let these gunslingers tread on them. None of them seems to have any fight left in him. And the ranchers are no better. I've seen more than a dozen of them come and go, herded out of the territory like cattle by this woman and her hirelings. How much longer are they going to take it lying down?'

'That's something I can't answer,' said Bart sombrely. 'But at least, I may be able to do something about it. You said you knew where that evidence might lie. If you tell me, I may be able to lay my hands on it. Once Zena Clayburne knows that we have it, she may think twice about doing anything for fear of it coming out into the open. I've a feeling that she doesn't want too much bad publicity at the moment.'

'What makes you think that?' inquired the other, sitting up and taking notice.

Bart laughed. Now, for some odd reason he found that he could forget the aches and pains in his bruised body. He had the chance to strike back and that was all he asked at the moment. 'Because she let slip the fact that there have been some lawmen on her trail during the past few months. She seemed to think I might be one of them. That's why she went to so much trouble to try to get me out of the way. A couple of her hired hands were to ride me off the spread, but on the way I was to meet with an unfortunate accident. Trouble was, I was ready for them and she's now two hands short. I reckon she probably knows about it by now and she'll be wondering just what happened to them, and more particularly what happened to me.'

The other stared across the table at him and there was a glint at the back of his eyes that had not been there before.

'You know, young fella,' he said admiringly. 'I always did like a man with spunk and you seem to be that man. I reckon if it's possible at all to get those documents and papers, you might be the one to do it. You handy with a gun?'

'Sure. If I had one. They took mine when I bumped into them this morning.'

'I've got a couple stacked away in my drawer, all ready for use,' said the other quietly. He rose to his feet, caught Bart's sudden glance towards the ancient weapon that rested on the table and shook his head with a hard, bitter laugh. 'They ain't nothing like that. These are real guns that belonged to a real man. I reckon if he were here today, he'd be proud for you to wear them.' He walked across the room and unlocked a drawer in the desk in the far corner. Pulling out a heavy gunbelt, he brought it across to Bart. 'Here you are. These belonged to one of my best friends. He used them to try to bring law and order to this town in the lawless days. He would have done it too, if he hadn't been shot in the back by a couple of murdering polecats working on Zena Clayburne's orders.'

'Sheriff Keene?' Bart glanced down at the guns in his hands for a moment in sudden surprise, then touched them gently with his fingers, pulling them from their holsters, liking the feel and balance of the smooth weapons, feeling the hard metal in his fingers. They were both loaded and he examined each chamber before flipping them back into place.

'That's right. There are some folk around here who seem to think he was a coward. They try to say that he was shot running away from those two critters. I did my best to publish what I knew to be the truth, tried to clear his name. That was when Zena Clayburne and Jeb Saunders, her right-hand killer, paid me a visit. They didn't leave me in any doubt as to what they would do if I printed anything like that again. Threatened to burn my paper and wreck the press.'

Bart nodded. For a moment, he hesitated, then rose slowly

to his feet, holding the belt in his hand.

'Put them on, Bart,' said the other quietly. 'They're yours now. Use them as he would want them to be used. Go ahead.'

Bart hesitated for a moment longer, then unstrapped his own empty gunbelt from around his waist and buckled the other into place. They fitted as if they had belonged there all of his life. He rested his fingertips on the butts for a moment, getting the feel of them, then nodded, satisfied. He studied the other for a moment, then said quickly: 'Tell me what you know, Ben. There isn't much time and we have to move fast.'

'Time for something to eat and drink and a wash for that battered face of yours, and then we'll talk,' said the other soberly, 'The night is still young and you won't be able to do anything until the town quietens. If you're seen here, there'll be all hell to pay. The sheriff and a band of gunslammers have been riding the hills to the south looking for you. They reckoned that you must have headed in that direction after you broke out of jail. They also reckon that Tess and her father had something to do with the jailbreak, but they can't prove anything and at the moment, they ain't trying. All they want to do is get their hands on you, and you'll swing from the first tree they find. They won't take any more chances with you, the next time they lay their hands on you.'

'So I gathered.' Bart nodded and remembered the bunch of men he had seen riding hell for leather towards the Clayburne spread. Sheriff Jason and his posse going to inform her that their mission to the south had been a failure? It seemed more than likely now.

He seated himself at the table with a show of ill-concealed impatience and waited while the other brought out food and hot coffee from the room at the rear of the building. He placed them on the table, then acting on impulse, went back and returned with a slender, tall-necked bottle. 'I figure we may as well drink,' he said by way of explanation. 'Who knows, it may be the last time for either of us and it's been waiting there too long for an occasion such as this.'

He poured some of the rich amber liquid into two glasses which he had brought with him and pushed one of them towards Bart. 'Eat up,' he said quietly, 'we can talk at the same time.'

Bart nodded. For the first time since that morning, he realized just how hungry and thirsty he really was. Gradually, the gnawing hunger pains in the pit of his stomach went away and he glanced inquiringly at the man who sat opposite him, the man who had tried to wage a single-handed war against Zena Clayburne.

'Go ahead,' he said quietly. 'Where are these documents you talk about?'

'They're in the safe inside Jason's office. Zena Clayburne keeps them there for safe keeping.'

'Just what are they? Have you seen them yourself?'

'Nope. All I know is what Keene told me before he died. He had a hunch that something might happen to him and he warned me about them. Seems the deeds to the Clayburne ranch aren't legal and there are also papers that Keene got from somewheres concerning the ranches that she took over when she bought out the mortgages from the banks. They ain't legal either.'

'I see. Then if that's so, why didn't they destroy them as soon as they got their hands on them.'

'That's something only Zena Clayburne knows. Reckon that Jason wouldn't mind having them burnt right now. But she says – no. They stay there until she's good and ready. Reckons it gives her a feeling of power just to know that they are there and if the townsfolk knew they'd do anything to try to get them back.'

'You mean that nobody in town knows about them?'

'That's right. Only Sheriff Jason, Zena and myself. And they don't know that I'm wise to them either.'

Bart tightened his lips. He drained the liquor in the glass, felt the warm haze inside his stomach. His grey eyes were cold as he stood up. 'I'll get those papers.' he promised. 'And you can use them in your paper tomorrow. Reckon this is going to be one edition the likes of which this town ain't seen in many a year.'

'The reactions are going to be interesting,' admitted Ben. 'But you're right. With those documents in our hand, we stand a far better chance of swinging things in our favour.'

'If that was the sheriff I spotted riding out to see Miss Clayburne, I ought to have the place to myself,' mused Bart. He went towards the door, paused with his hand on the handle as Wheeler said quietly, urgently: 'Not that way, Bart. They may have men watching the street. Go out the way you came, through the back and into the alley. And whatever you do, watch yourself. That might have been Jason you saw, but there are still plenty of killers loose in the town, looking for trouble, and in particular, looking for you.'

'I'll be careful,' Bart promised. He went swiftly along the narrow passage and out through the door which led into the dark alley. Nothing moved out there in the darkness and he paused for a moment, checking the guns at his waist, before easing himself forward, hugging the back of the buildings, keeping into the long shadows as much as possible.

Behind him, he heard the door close with a soft sound that was lost almost at once. At the end of the alley, his mount still stood where he had left it. Evidently, no one knew that he was back in town. Sweeping his eyes from side to side, his head well down, face hidden beneath the wide brim of his shapeless hat, he walked softly along the darkened boardwalk, one hand hovering close to the butt of the Colt. A bullet could come from any of the shadowed alleyways or the windows that overlooked the street. For all he knew there might be a hundred guns lined up on him at that very moment, a hundred itchy fingers on the triggers, each ready to blast him into eternity.

But he knew that at the first sign of hesitation he would give himself away completely to any gunman who might be watching him. He could only continue along the street in the direction of the sheriff's office, hoping that he could reach there before he was seen, and that Jason and his deputies were still out of town. There seemed to be an emptiness, a frigidity, about the town as he paused in front of the sheriff's office, in front of the jailhouse. A quick glance up and down the dusty street was sufficient to tell him that although the saloons were still packed, there was no one around watching him. He went forward with a cat-like tread, feet soundless on the boardwalk. There was a warning bell ringing sharply at the back of his brain, but he forced himself to ignore it. Everything looked too simple, too quiet, for it to be anything but a trap; but that was a chance that he had to take if he was to go through with this. He had managed to get this far without running into trouble and now he was armed.

Cautiously, he skirted around the building, pulling one of the heavy Colts noiselessly from its holster and holding it balanced in his right hand, finger on the trigger. There was no sound from inside the darkened office and although no light showed this only served to heighten the tension which was building up in his mind. At the rear of the building, he found an open window and raised it slowly. It squeaked a little and he paused for a moment, his heart hammering in the base of his throat, but the sound had passed unnoticed. The small room beyond was silent and empty.

Within seconds, he was inside, moving across to the closed door which he guessed might lead out into the passage fronting the cells. It did, and he realized that he had been wrong earlier when he had fled from this place, thinking that there was only one way out. There was the glint of steel in his eyes as he opened the door, made his way along the passage. It was the work of a few moments, to find his way into the office. The shutters were already in place over the windows and he struck a sulphur match and lit the lantern on the desk. The small safe was just where Wheeler had said it would be, tucked away in one corner, set in the wall itself.

Once he had opened the panel in the wall, he found that

inside, the safe itself lay open. By the flickering light of the lantern he made out the papers which had been pushed tightly into the back and pulled them out swiftly, taking them over to the desk to examine them more closely. Finally, he was satisfied. Wheeler had certainly not exaggerated when he had considered these documents to be important. They showed, beyond any shadow of doubt, that the Clayburne place, which had originally belonged to a man named Jedburn, had been willed to his son on his father's death, but that the son had never come forward to claim his inheritance. It had then been transferred to Zena Clayburne and the name at the bottom of the document was that of Sheriff Jason. There was little doubt that the two had been in cahoots even then, thought Bart fiercely. He riffled through the other papers there, then paused and read through them again. Slowly, the picture was beginning to take shape.

It was all there, kept in the safe because of some warped sense of triumph on the part of Zena Clayburne. He wondered if she ever came here to gloat over the story which these documents told. How Chuck Jedburn had been shot down in a duel in the main street of Cochita City some seven months after Zena Clayburne had taken over the ranch and the herd. There had been no doubt that it had been sheer, cold-blooded murder, that the man who had gunned down the boy had been a professional gunman, hired by Miss Clayburne.

Carefully, he placed the papers into his shirt, closed the safe and pushed the desk back into place in front of it. Once copies of these were printed, it would go a long way towards defeating these killers and returning the herds which had been rustled to their rightful owners, together with all of the land that had been stolen. Going back to the desk, he bent to blow out the lights, then paused.

In the street outside, he picked out the unmistakable sound of men riding hard into town from the north end of the street. Fifteen, possibly twenty men, he estimated.

Bending swiftly, he blew out the lamp, leaving the room in darkness. The riders stopped in front of the jailhouse and he heard the murmur of voices as they swung themselves down out of the saddle. Sheriff Jason and the posse! He backed away to the far side of the room, opened the door which led out into the passage and slipped back through it, leaving it slightly ajar. Almost without direction, his fingers loosened the guns in his holsters. He ran a dry tongue over equally dry lips and waited. Footsteps sounded on the veranda outside. There was a pause and then the outer door was thrust roughly open and through the crack Bart made out the fat figure of Sheriff Jason as he came into the office, walked up to the desk and lit the lamp. He slumped down into the chair behind the desk and ran his hand over the stubble on his chin. Three men came in after him and stood for a moment, staring down at him. All three looked more like professional killers than deputies and Bart guessed that they had been deliberately hired by Zena Clayburne and ordered to ride with the sheriff.

'Tell the rest of the boys to stable their horses, and get something to eat and drink.' said Jason thickly. 'After all of that riding, they'll need it. I say that he never rode south at all. He probably went north, up into the mountains, probably knows this is the last place we'd think of looking for him.'

One of the men nodded and went out. Reaching into the drawer behind his desk, Jason pulled out a bottle of whiskey and poured a slug into each of three glasses, nodding to the men. He sighed and leaned back in his chair, tilting the glass in his hand, then he lifted the brimming rim to his lips and drank, not taking it away until all of the whiskey was finished. There was dust on his jacket and ingrained into the folds of his face.

Bart eyed him closely from his hiding place. The others had ridden hard all of that day and on a fruitless chase. He guessed that they had just returned from reporting failure to Zena Clayburne and that would not have left them in any better frame of mind. He checked the guns at his waist and

100

debated whether to step into the room and take on all three of them while he had the chance. He might never get another opportunity like this, he reflected inwardly. Then he remembered the rest of the men outside somewhere across at the livery stable and knew that they would all come running once they heard any gunplay in the sheriff's office and there were those precious papers in his jacket to take care of. At the moment, he could not afford to allow himself to be killed. There was far too much at stake now. It was more than his life against the whole of the mighty Clayburne organization. It meant the life of an entire town, of a decent way of life for the people who lived here; people who, at the moment, did not seem to think it worth while fighting for.

For an instant, the bitterness lay deep within him. Was this what Dodson and the other members of that trailing herd had died for? he wondered. So that men like these could run wild in the town. He held a tight grip on himself. A moment later, the door to the office swung open again and a tall man stepped into the room. Bart felt the muscles of his chest tighten spasmodically as he caught a glimpse of the other's face in the light of the lantern. This was the face he knew he would never forget as long as either of them lived. The black-bearded man he had last seen in an exploding red haze of pain on top of the redstone bluffs just before he toppled thirty feet or so, down the sheer face of the cliff. The man that Wheeler had called Jeb Saunders, Zena Clayburne's right-hand killer.

For a moment, the urge to step into that room with guns blazing was almost more than he could restrain. Savagely, he fought it down, knowing that to do so would be taking far too great a risk. There was little doubt that he could take all of these men before they knew he was there, but he couldn't fight the others and he had to get back to Wheeler with this information. There would come another time, some place, when this man would stand in front of him again.

'The others think that it would be useless to ride south

again tomorrow,' said Saunders thickly. He picked up the bottle from the desk and poured himself a glass without even looking at Jason. Bart noticed the gesture instantly and filed it away for future reference. There was no love lost between these two men, he decided. It was something he might be able to exploit in the future.

'You heard what Miss Clayburne said, Jeb,' muttered the other harshly. 'She gives the orders around here as far as I'm concerned. She thinks he's to the south, so that's the way we go. You'd better tell them so.'

The other seated himself on one corner of the desk, one leg swinging idly. 'Do you reckon that he's still alive, Jason?'

The sheriff looked up and there was a startled look on his flabby features. 'If he ain't, then why is she in such a goddurned tizzy?' he demanded.

'I'm not sure. She's been mighty tight-lipped lately, but while we were there I heard from one of the hands that some *hombre* rode in this morning asking for a job and that Jake and Clem took him for a ride off the spread. So far, it appears none of them came back.'

'So?' There was a new note in Jason's deep voice. 'You figure that it was Shannon who rode in this morning?'

'Could be. He's supposed to be a fast man with a gun and we know that he's looking fer trouble. Ever since we heard he was holed up with the Guthries, I knew we'd get trouble from him. That's why I said we ought to have ridden out then and taken care of him. But she wouldn't hear of it. You reckon that she's getting soft, Jason?'

'Now you ain't got no cause to go talking like that, Saunders.' The portly sheriff heaved himself to his feet and stood with his hands resting flat on the top of the desk. For a moment, there was an electric silence in the room, a tautness that could be felt. Then both men relaxed visibly and the tension was broken. 'Besides,' went on Jason slowly. 'There are still those papers, you know. If they should get into the wrong hands, and the townsfolk heard you were the man who

102

shot Sheriff Keene in the back as he came out of the saloon, it might have a very unfortunate effect.'

'You talk too much, Jason,' snarled the other. He slid his legs to the floor and walked towards the door. 'One day, you'll say a little too much and if I'm around when you do—' He deliberately left the rest of the threat unsaid, but Bart noticed the sudden tightening of Jason's lips, saw the way his fingers curled on the top of the desk, and knew that the threat had struck home.

But at least this told him why Zena Clayburne had been so anxious to keep those papers. They were her one guarantee that these killers would do as she said, otherwise the whole sordid story would come out into the open. He leaned back again and watched Jason. Even though this man seemingly held the whip-hand here, he had the impression that he would be one of the first of these killers to crack.

The other two men finished their drinks. Jason poured himself another, nodded towards the bottle, but the men shook their heads. 'It's been a hard day, Sheriff,' said one of them. 'Reckon I'll hit the hay. We've an even longer ride ahead of us tomorrow.' He paused, then went on slowly, 'But I reckon Jeb might have been right, you know. This *hombre* Shannon could be dead by now, especially if he was that critter who rode in this morning.'

'He could be,' said Jason heavily. He pulled his huge body up higher in the chair. 'But when you work for anyone like Miss Clayburne you have to make sure.'

He gulped down the drink, sat and watched as the two men turned on their heel and went out, closing the door behind them. Bart could hear the sound of their footsteps on the wooden boardwalk outside, fading into the distance. Then the room was silent, with only Jason sitting at the desk, his eyes just beginning to glaze, as he poured a third drink from the bottle and sat for a long moment, staring down at the liquid sloshing around in the glass. Abruptly, he set the glass down on the desk, spilling some of the liquid as he rose

103

a trifle unsteadily to his feet. Lurching to the door, he turned the key in the lock and shot the thick bolt into place, before going back and settling down in the chair again.

The glass was halfway to his lips when Bart pushed the door open silently and stepped into the room. For a moment, Jason stared across the room at him, his mouth hanging slackly open, eyes wide and staring as if he were looking at a ghost. Then he gulped down the remaining liquid in the glass and set it down with a hand that trembled violently.

'Shannon!' The single word was almost an accusation. He sat like a man carved from stone, unable to move, his face rigid. 'I thought you were— They said that you had ridden out—' He stopped again and made a quick dive for the bottle. He seemed to have forgotten that he was wearing guns and that he was the sheriff of the town – or perhaps, thought Bart grimly, he had heard of his reputation and did not intend to commit suicide by trying to outdraw him in fair fight.

'Drink up,' said Bart quietly. He strode forward. 'It may be the last you'll have, so make the most of it.'

'What do you want with me, Shannon?' protested the other whiningly. 'If it's because of what happened a couple of days ago, I can explain all of that. I had to bring you in, you see that, don't you? As the law around here, I had to ride out and get you when that warrant was sworn out for your arrest. There was nothing else I could do. My hands were tied and—'

Bart smiled thinly. 'And you figured that, once you heard I'd ridden off with Clem and Jake, Zena Clayburne's two killers, you'd be quite safe.' He shook his head. 'As you see, they didn't do their job properly either. I'm still here and I intend to smash you and your whole rotten set-up.'

Jason finished the whiskey in the glass and drew a deep breath into his lungs. His eyes were bright in the light of the lantern and they were never still. Then he leaned back and ran the tip of his tongue over dry lips. 'You aiming to shoot me out of hand, Shannon?' He was desperately trying to get some of his courage back, possibly realizing that any shot here would instantly rouse the entire town.

'That's all you deserve,' grated Bart. He touched the guns at his waist, saw the sweat start out on the other's forehead. 'I reckon that it would be justice to kill you with Sheriff Keene's guns.' A tight smile hovered around his lips as he saw the other's eyes widen. 'That's right, the man you had shot in the back by Saunders. It wasn't wise of you, or Zena Clayburne to keep those papers.' He saw the other's gaze flick suddenly to the far corner of the room. 'That's right, they aren't there any longer. I have them and I intend to see that they get into the right hands. And when I do, I'll bust you and those outlaw killers right open.'

'Don't fool yourself, Shannon. You don't stand a chance around here – and you know it. Why be like this anyway? So you lost your herd. That's a good reason for feeling sore, I reckon. But I'm sure that if I had a word with Miss Clayburne, there might be a place for you in her outfit. She's always on the look out for a man who can handle a gun.'

Bart smiled grimly. 'I asked for a job like that this morning, and she wasn't interested. Seemed to think I had to be killed. I don't aim to put my head in a noose a second time. Besides—' His voice hardened deliberately, 'I made a vow to kill those men who rustled that herd. Now that I know for sure who they are, I'm going to carry it through.'

'By yourself?' There was a faint flicker of contempt on the other's fleshy features. 'Or mebbe you figure on the Guthries helping you. They won't be able to do anything, Shannon. One word from Miss Clayburne and they'll be run off the range and they know it. Take my advice and get outa town while you still have the chance. Otherwise, use that gun. You'll kill me but you'll be dead before you make it across the street.'

Bart eyed the other closely. The man was bluffing. He knew that he would not use the gun there, but he was still

105

afraid for himself and Bart was banking on that fear to help him.

'I don't aim to kill you here, Jason,' he said thinly. 'That would be a fool thing to do. But I'm taking you with me, just as a guarantee that your men won't try anything funny.'

For a moment, there was a flicker of fear in the other's eyes as Bart leaned forward, prodding him in the chest with the barrel of the gun. 'On your feet, Jason. You and I are going to take a little ride, with these papers that you've been keeping so vigilantly in your office all this time. I'm sure that a friend of mine will find them extremely interesting.'

'If you think you can make me go with you, you're wrong, Shannon. I've only got to shout for help and there'll be a score of men bursting in here.'

'Mebbe so, but you won't hear them,' promised Bart with a threat in his voice. 'Now get on your feet. You're as big a sidewinding killer as the others and it won't need much for me to pull this trigger. I ought to shoot you down in cold blood here and now, but I figure you may come in handy later. That's the only reason I'm sparing your life.'

Jason looked up and his cheeks were flushed, his eyes bright. For a moment, he hesitated, then stumbled drunkenly to his feet. There was a sullen look on his face and he fell heavily against the desk as he tried to stand upright. Bart stepped back a couple of paces, moving around the side of the desk and it was at that moment, that Jason suddenly plucked up courage from somewhere and made his play. He did not go for the guns in his belt as Bart had half expected him to do. Instead, he threw himself sideways, the whole of his weight slamming against the desk. In spite of its weight, it tilted over against Bart and he moved instinctively. Out of the corner of his eye, he saw the other coming at him, his face alive with a ferocious anger, mingled with fear. The sheriff knew now that he was fighting for his life. Bracing himself, Bart took the other's bull-headed rush against his side. Jason's hands were clawing for his wrist, forcing it up, thrusting the gun back and away. With an effort, Bart released his pressure on the trigger, knowing that more than anything else, the other wanted him to fire that shot, knowing that the bullet would bury itself in the ceiling and not in his fat carcass, and that the noise of the shot would bring help from every quarter.

Struggling with the other, Bart chopped downwards with his free hand. The heel of his palm slipped off the other's jowl and he staggered back, swallowing convulsively, his adam's apple bobbing up and down as he tried to suck air into his lungs through his semi-paralysed throat. The muscles of his neck corded and constricted as he fought for breath. His grip on Bart's wrist relaxed and with a sudden wrench Bart brought his arm down, reversed the gun in his hand and laid the barrel across the other's shoulder, close to the neck. It was a stunning blow, inflicting more pain than injury. Jason yelped hoarsely and went down on to one knee. He swayed for a moment, trying to maintain a hold on his consciousness. His eyes were glazed slightly and there was blood on his puffy features.

Bart drew himself upright and stood for a long moment, listening intently. Outside, there came a yell of coarse laughter from the direction of the nearby saloon, but that was all. A horse snickered faintly a moment later, but there was no sound of footsteps on the boardwalk running forward to investigate the noise.

Evidently the men who had ridden out with Jason had taken his orders literally and were now in the saloons, eating and drinking, washing the dust of the trail out of their throats with hard liquor. Any slight ruckus from the direction of the sheriff's office had passed unnoticed. 'Get on to your feet,' snapped Bart tightly. 'Any more funny stuff and I'll kill you. It may help me to have you alive, but I'd just as soon leave you here dead in the hope that the people of Cochita City will elect themselves a straight-shooting sheriff.'

Jason did not need to be told twice. Gasping with the

107

effort, he stood up, leaning on the edge of the desk to keep his balance. He worked his jaw for a moment experimentally, wincing whenever his fingers touched a tender, bruised spot. There was hate in his eyes as he stared across at Bart. 'I'll remember this, Shannon,' he said hoarsely, finding difficulty in speaking through his bruised vocal chords. 'I'll get you and kill you myself if it's the last thing I do.'

'Just walk out of here slowly and give me no trouble, or it may be the last thing you'll do,' promised Bart grimly. 'You don't deserve dying easy with a bullet. If I thought that you'd hang for what you've done, along with Saunders and the other gunslingers, I'd leave it up to the conscience of the decent citizens of this town to deal with you. But I can't be sure that you wouldn't get out of it, just as you've got out of so many things in the past.'

For a moment, he had the impression that the other intended to make a move for his guns, but he shrugged aside the insult and stepped towards the door.

'Open it real slow,' warned Bart. 'Better make sure there are none of your men there before you—' He broke off sharply. There was the sound of heavy footsteps on the boardwalk outside, coming swiftly closer. They paused outside the door and a moment later, there was the sound of someone rapping heavily on it.

'Be careful what you say,' warned Bart in a hissed whisper. 'I'll be right behind you with this gun in my hand.' He prodded the other with the gun in the small of the back. 'And I'll be listening real close. Ask who it is?'

'Who is it?' Jason was now taking no chances with the desperate man at his back.

'Matson, Sheriff. You asked me to come back after I'd stabled the horses.'

Jason hesitated and Bart jabbed the gun into his back again, saw the look of pain flash over the other's face, the beading of sweat on his forehead and the sudden look of fear in his eyes. 'Tell him you won't need him any more tonight.

You'll see him in the morning,' he ordered.

Jason swallowed convulsively, licked his dry lips for a moment, his mouth moving but no sound coming out. Then he seemed to find his voice. 'Everything will be all right tonight, Ben. Jest you go on over to the saloon and enjoy yourself. I'll see you in the morning.'

A pause, then: 'Suits me, Sheriff' The footsteps sounded again, retreating into the street.

'All right, now walk in front of me, slow and easy.' Bart eyed the other coldly, remembering everything he had heard about this crooked sheriff who ran the town for Lena Clayburne, the man who had ridden out to arrest him on a trumped up charge of murder and he wished that he could pull the trigger at that moment, so that he could be perfectly sure. But that kind of killing wasn't possible right now. He would have to bide his time. Going up behind the other, he slipped the sheriff's guns from their holsters and tossed them into one corner of the room.

'Now walk down the steps slow and easy,' Bart said. 'And if one of your boys steps out for some air, tell him that you're taking me in by yourself. If they make a wrong move, you get it first, Savvy?'

Jason nodded quickly. He stepped out into the quiet street, paused for a moment, then walked quickly along it, Bart close on his heels. They walked past the saloon with its lights glaring inside. The batwing doors were closed, but as they came up to them, they swung open and two men spilled out into the street. Both were drunk and fell sprawling into the gutter, their arms flung out ahead of them. One pulled himself up and sat staring at Bart and his prisoner through bleary eyes. There was no recognition in them and Bart knew he could expect no trouble from that quarter. But the other man was not quite as drunk as his companion and he lurched upright, swaying forward, holding on to the wooden upright for support.

'Where are you going to at this time of night, Sheriff?' he

drawled thickly. 'Come inside. The drinks are on me.'

Bart shook his head before the other could reply. 'Not tonight, friend. We have important business out of town. Tomorrow mebbe.'

The other shrugged, then lurched away down the street. Prodding the other forward again, Bart forced him along the main street until they were directly opposite the small, dingy place where Ben Wheeler tried to publish the truth in Cochita City. For a moment, Jason looked back at him in surprise as they halted.

'Why did you bring me here?' he demanded thinly. 'There's nothing here and—'

'We'll just go inside and have a nice quiet talk,' suggested Bart tightly, almost as if he had not heard the interruption. He rapped loudly on the door, waited while the bolt was pulled back. A moment later, it opened an inch and he saw Wheeler's face peering out at him through the crack. The door opened further as the other saw who it was.

'Brought someone along to see you,' Bart said, as he thrust the sheriff into the room. 'Reckon he might be able to help us a great deal.'

'Do you think that was wise?' queried the other. He eyed Jason with a mixture of loathing and fear. 'If his men should discover that he's missing and come looking for him.'

'They don't know where to find him and if he makes one sound, it'll be his last,' Bart warned. He motioned Jason into the seat directly opposite him at the small table, letting himself down into his own chair carefully, his eyes never leaving the other's face, keeping his gun trained on the sheriff's middle. Jason was sweating profusely. He pulled out a large red handkerchief and mopped his brow.

'I thought you would have had more sense than to associate with men like this low-down killer,' said Jason thinly, glancing out of the corner of his eye in Wheeler's direction. 'Especially after what happened the last time. Believe me, it can quite easily happen again.'

110

'Seems to me that you're doing a mite lot of talking for a man with a gun trained on him,' Bart pointed out. He jerked his head towards Wheeler. 'I got those documents you were talking about, Ben. Reckon they're the real McCoy. You ought to be able to use this information in that sheet of yours tomorrow.'

Jason strained forward in his chair as Bart took the papers from inside his jacket and handed them over to the editor. Ben Wheeler took them and walked over to the desk, sitting down where the light fell full upon them as he went through them carefully. There was a taut, strained silence in the room now as Wheeler read the papers through carefully, not once looking up until he had finished. Then he laid them down slowly on his desk and stared across at Bart. 'I knew these documents were dynamite, but I never expected anything like this. It's odd that Zena Clayburne should have kept them. They would have been far safer destroyed than locked away, even in a safe like that.'

Jason licked his lips, leaning forward in the chair, suddenly unsure of himself. 'You don't really believe a word that's in them, do you?' He guffawed harshly, trying to force evenness into his voice. 'Lies, every word of them.'

Wheeler looked at him tightly for a long moment over the steel-rimmed spectacles, then shook his head. 'You don't fool me for one minute, Jason,' he said. 'If Zena Clayburne knew that we had these, she'd send every man she has into town to get them back before we can let the townsfolk and ranchers know how they've been swindled.'

The sweat was running down Jason's forehead now. He'd lost his look of assuredness. The muscles of his face worked under the sallow skin and he seemed to be straining in the chair as if against invisible bonds.

'If you print that story, you'll never live to see another sundown,' he snarled viciously. 'I'm warning you, Wheeler. Think twice before you print that. You know what happened the last time you fell foul of Zena Clayburne. That won't be anything compared to what you'll get tomorrow.'

Bart opened his mouth to reply to the other, but before he could say anything, Ben Wheeler had risen to his feet and was standing in front of the sheriff. He said with a glacial calmness, 'I've taken all the evil and rottenness that I can from the people who run this town, Jason. I've sat by here, helpless, while you and Zena Clayburne have fleeced the ranchers, rustled herds from the main trails through to Abilene, and killed road agents and Pinkerton men. Yes, I know all about those murders too, Jason, and this time, I intend to see that something is done about them.'

'You're a goddurned fool,' hissed the other. 'It's this man who's put you up to it. There's no reason that you and the other should suffer just because he's trying to get even with us for rustling his herd.'

'Sheriff.' The other spat the solitary word out. 'I'm not merely concerned with a herd that's been rustled. I'm concerned with the men who shot Sheriff Keene in the back and elected you to take his place. You ain't worthy to be in his boots, and by God, I'm going to see that you don't stay in them much longer.'

'You're loco,' snapped the other. 'You can say all you want, but nothing is going to change the fact that once Zena Clayburne hears about this, you and this gunslick will be strung up from the nearest tree or shot down in the street. Then Cochita City will see just how easily you can protect them.'

Wheeler shrugged and went back to the press in the middle of the room. He began setting up the type, his nimble fingers moving quickly as he worked, his face rapt in concentration. Bart seated himself in the chair again and kept an eye on Jason. He hadn't quite made up his mind what to do about the other. Certainly he could not afford to leave him here in Cochita City and it would be dangerous to leave him with Wheeler. The other was old and could not handle a gun now. Besides, once the sheriff was missed and this new edition of the town paper came out on to the streets, all hell might be let loose. The sooner he got the sheriff well away from town, somewhere where he could do no further harm, the better he would feel.

He wondered whether or not it would be safe to take him out to the Guthrie place and ask them to keep a watch over him until things came to the inevitable showdown. They were far enough from the town to keep him out of trouble and he knew that he could trust them implicitly.

'Need any help, Ben?' he asked eventually, once all of the type had been set up. 'Reckon the sheriff here is just itching to help get this particular edition printed, aren't you, Jason?'

The other cringed under the implied threat in Bart's voice. 'I ain't having no part in this,' he snarled. In spite of his tone, he was obviously flustered.

'No?' Bart raised his brows slightly. 'Get on your feet and help Ben.' He jerked the barrel of the gun in the direction of the press. 'There's a lot to be done and we have to be well away from here by sun-up.'

It was Jason's turn to look surprised. 'You figure on killing me somewhere away from town then?'

'Perhaps. Now work that press.'

Reluctantly, the other got to his feet and shuffled over to where the old man was busy working the heavy press. At Bart's orders, Jason took over from him and soon, more sweat was streaming down his face than ever before. Bart eyed him dispassionately. His mind was cold with an anger that would not surface, as cold and hard and as lethal as the gun that continued to point at the sheriff. For almost an hour, the other was forced to work the heavy machinery of the press until Wheeler was satisfied that they had printed sufficient sheets. When he was finished. Jason sank down into the chair, arms hanging loosely by his sides.

'Reckon it isn't easy for folk like you to do any honest work,' said Bart thinly. He paused for a moment, while Wheeler checked everything; then when the other gave a

113

quick nod, he gestured Jason to his feet. 'I'll take this side-winder out of town, Ben,' he said slowly, deliberately. 'We'll be miles away by sun-up and if any of his posse are thinking of following us, I reckon we can handle them.'

'You're certain that you don't need me to ride along with you, Bart?' asked the other. 'I may be old, but I can still handle a gun.'

'Nope,' Bart sounded decisive. 'I need you here. But what-ever happens, be careful. Once those sheets hit the streets, they'll try to come gunning for you.'

'I'll be careful. What do you intend to do with Jason here?'

'I reckon I'll take him out to a couple of friends of mine in the hills. They may know how to make him talk.' Bart's brows were wrinkled in thought. 'I've got a feeling that we don't know the whole truth yet. These papers say that Jeb Saunders killed Sheriff Keene by shooting him in the back as he stepped out of the saloon.'

'And you don't believe that?'

'No. It's all too easy and simple. I've a feeling there's some-thing more to it than that and I intend to find out.' He nodded in the direction of Jason. 'I think the worthy sheriff knows something that he hasn't told us yet. He'll deny it here, of course, and we may not be able to get it out of him. But there are some people who know ways of loosening a stub-born tongue.'

'You won't get me to talk,' snapped Jason. He tried to make himself sound brave and failed miserably.

Few men took more than casual notice of the two men as they rode along the main street of Cochita City during the early hours of that morning and took the trail that led to the south, through the buttes. A couple of drunks still lay in the gutter near the boardwalk and there was a light in the doctor's window, the only light in the whole of the street which showed without shutters being in front of the windows. Bart threw it a quick glance, then rode on with Jason in the saddle beside him, staring straight ahead. He could almost guess at the thoughts which were racing through the sheriff's mind at that very moment. He was trying desperately to figure out a way of escaping, before they got too far into the buttes where he was well away from any help from his own men or Zena Clayburne.

By dawn, they were well into the buttes, taking the valley trail, Bart riding a little way behind the other, his hand never far from the butt of his gun. With Jason in his hands, Bart no longer feared any men who might be watching the trail as much as he had in the past. It was still likely that any of Zena Clayburne's hired killers might open fire on him, even with the sheriff there, but that was a remote possibility. There was a grim smile on Bart's face as he rode with the wind in his face, feeling the cool, crisp scent of the country go down into his nostrils and enter his lungs. It would be a tremendous pity if all of this was to come under the control of one woman, and a vicious, murdering woman at that. A beautiful woman with the face of an angel and the heart of a devil. He remembered the way in which she had arranged for him to be killed and the utter cold-bloodedness of it sent a little shiver racing through him. What kind of a woman was she, anyway? he mused. There had to be something twisted inside her mind for her to act the way she did. A woman with greed uppermost in everything she did, utterly ruthless, as ready to kill anyone who stood in her way, as any man would have been.

They rode the low ridge which looked down on the valley, where the trail turned and then dipped down into the Guthrie spread. The first indication that there was anything wrong came when they reached the bend in the trail. Bart smelled the acrid smoke even before he turned the corner and could look down upon where the ranch had stood. Now there was nothing down there but a pile of glowing beams and spars, still smouldering in the bright sunlight. A pall of smoke hung heavily in the air and it was clear that the place had not been fired long before. He sat tall in the saddle for a long moment, looking down, scarcely able to take everything in. This shattered any hopes he might have had of keeping Jason here for security. But even this thought faded into insignificance beside the knowledge that both Tess and her father might have been killed when the outlaws had attacked this place and razed it to the ground. They seemed to have spared nothing and he knew with a sudden certainty that both Tess and her father would have stayed there and fought back, even against overwhelming odds.

'Looks like you're too late, Shannon,' said Jason sarcastically. He seemed to have regained a little of his composure at the sight below. 'You won't be able to keep me here now, will you? Why don't you get it into your thick skull that you're beaten, that you can't hope to win this one-sided battle you've started. Give up and take the advice I gave you. If you went in with Zena Clayburne, I could promise you you'll never regret it.'

Bart shook his head. His lips were drawn into a tight line across the middle of his face. 'Get down there,' he ordered sharply. His face was a terrible thing.

'If they've killed Tess and her father, then you won't leave this place alive. There'll be another victim here before I leave.'

Dismounting in front of the charred remains of the house, Bart felt a tight sickness in the pit of his stomach. From above, it had looked as though there might still have been a little of the building left standing, but from here, he saw that the devastation was complete. No one could possibly be still alive if they had been trapped in there, once the flames had taken hold. But this did not stop him from plunging into the ruins, searching underfoot for any sign of life. While he worked, Jason stood outside, in the blackened courtyard, watching him with veiled eyes, biding his time, waiting for a chance to break free.

Fifteen minutes later, Bart stepped out of the grey ashes, the dull sickness showing in his eyes. Jason grinned down at him, mopping his brow with the large red handkerchief, eyes glinting in the sunlight.

'You're a fool if you reckon they're still alive,' said Jason harshly. 'You see what happens to anyone who tries to go against Miss Clayburne. The same thing could quite easily happen to you. You might figure that I'm the law around these parts, but I'm not – she is. I only do what she says I have to do.'

'If there's one thing lower than a snake's belly, it's a crooked sheriff,' muttered Bart. He turned to throw one last look at the burnt ruins, and it was at that moment that Jason moved. Before Bart was aware of it, before he even guessed that the sight of what the outlaws had done here had been sufficient to slow down his reflexes to danger point, the other had pressed close, whipping one of the guns from its holster. Bart whirled swiftly, right hand snaking for the other gun at his waist, then froze.

'Hold it, Shannon, or I'll drop you now.' There was real menace in the sheriff's tone which stopped Bart in his tracks. He cursed himself for having been such a fool not to have kept a closer watch on the other. 'I'm afraid that I'm not quite as troubled by my conscience as you are. It doesn't worry me in the least to shoot an unarmed man down in cold blood. I shall leave your body here and spread it around that I caught the outlaws in the act of attacking this place. I was, unfortunately, too late to help anyone there, but I did manage to catch you before you escaped. Somehow, I don't think my story will be disbelieved. And if that fool of an editor has tried to put that paper on the streets, he'll be dead before sunset.' He smiled triumphantly. 'You weren't very smart after all, were you?'

Bart stared at the other in the harsh, glaring sunlight, knew that there was the promise of death in the sheriff's eyes and realized that he intended to use the gun at any moment. He was merely savouring the moment, prolonging it, before he squeezed the trigger.

For another instant, Jason gazed at him and then a flash of ferocious joy illuminated the dark, close-set eyes. Bart's hand went down in a fast draw, striking for his gun with the speed of a rattler, but even as his hand moved, he knew that he would never make it. He saw the small black hole in the other's barrel line up on his chest. Every little detail seemed to be drawn out in time as if it were taking place in slow motion. He tensed his body for the shuddering impact when the barrel spat flame. His own gun was clear of its holster, lifting on to its target, when the shot sounded. He flinched, then stared as though unable to believe his eyes as Jason sagged at the knees, shocked disbelief frozen on to his fleshy features, the eyes wide and staring, his head trying desperately to turn away from Bart, in the direction from which that shot had come so unexpectedly. His hands clutched automatically at the hole which had suddenly appeared in his chest, the blood beginning to soak into his shirt in a widening stain. Then he lurched forward, his face hitting the hard ground of the courtyard. His body jerked and toppled for a moment, then lay still. Out of the corner of his eye, Bart caught the sudden movement among the trees fifty feet away. He turned quickly, hand still on the gun, ready to jerk it up and fire in a split second.

Old Guthrie came out into the opening, holding the high-powered rifle in his right hand; behind him, came Tess. Guthrie turned the dead body of the sheriff over with the toe of his boot, stared down at the puffy face for a long moment with his lips drawn back into a sneer, then said softly: 'At least we won't have to bother with him now. Cochita City is without a sheriff, though they don't know it yet.'

'Reckon that you showed up just in time,' said Bart, relaxing a little. 'I thought you'd been killed when this happened.' He gestured towards the smouldering building, behind him.

Tess shook her head. 'We heard them riding this way and guessed why they were coming. They must have known that we had helped you. When you rode in a little while ago, we spotted the sheriff, but didn't recognize you. We were going to hide out in the brush there until you'd gone and then head into Cochita City. There's nothing left for us out here and in town, we may be able to help against Zena Clayburne.'

'Things are already moving in town,' said Bart. Quickly, he told them of what had happened, of the papers that had been found in the sheriff's safe, and the small newspaper that Wheeler had printed.

CHAPTER VI

GUNFIGHT IN COCHITA CITY

Night reached in from the east and there was a cold wind blowing off the prairie and down the rising ridges of the buttes. Bart shivered a little and pulled the collar of his jacket higher about his neck. They had buried Sheriff Jason beside the house which the outlaws he had allowed to ride free in the territory had pillaged and destroyed. For a long moment, Bart stood looking down at Guthrie. 'You still reckon you'd like to be in on the fight?' he asked tightly. He knew the answer before he asked the question.

'Shore would,' nodded the other. He gripped his rifle more tightly. 'But do yuh reckon we stand a chance?'

'A slim one. That's where Tess comes in.' He turned. 'Do you think you could ride out to Fort Apache and give this letter to the commander there. It should tell him enough of what's happening here for him to send some troops. Without them, we won't stand much of a chance. Colonel Elston is an old friend of mine. He'll come once he gets that letter. Better take the river trail, it's quicker. If you push your horse, you ought to make it before dawn and there shouldn't be any of

Miss Clayburne's men on that trail. They'll steer clear of the Fort.'

'I'll get through,' said the girl spiritedly. A few moments later, she swung herself agilely into the saddle of Jason's mount, pulled its head around and galloped off along the trail into the darkness.

'I hope that she makes it all right,' said Bart tightly. 'Without the help of the troops, we may never make it.'

'What do you figure on doing right now?' asked Guthrie. 'There ain't much point in staying on around here.'

With no change of expression, Bart said quietly: 'We'll have to get back into town. By now, Zena Clayburne will know what Ben Wheeler has been doing and if he's to stay alive, he'll need help.'

'You reckon they'll come to destroy that press like they threatened before?'

'Worse'n that, I figure they'll do their darnedest to kill him. That way, they'll be sure nothing like that is ever printed again.' His voice had an edge to it. 'Afraid that we won't make very good time with the two of us on the same mount, but it's either that or one will have to walk.'

They rode as quickly as they could, back along the trail, over the mesa and into Cochita City. It was still dark, with dawn another three hours away, but there were lights in the main street as they approached. Lights and the sound of gunfire which reached out to them as they came in from the south. The tightness knotted inside Bart. His hand gripped the reins more tightly at the sound. Were they too late? Had Zena Clayburne's men already arrived in town, and in force?

He gigged the mount forward, then slid from the saddle among the long shadows around the low shacks at the very edge of town. Very carefully, they made their way forward. There were lights showing through the windows of the three saloons and in those of the hotel. From the livery stable came the sound of horses chomping at their bits or kicking wildly at the sound. Darkness lay on the edges of the street where the actual gunplay seemed to he taking place, a dense darkness that was lit only intermittently by the flashes from the gun muzzles that sent glowing sparks across the darkness.

'That's Ben Wheeler's place all right,' murmured Guthrie. He moved forward without a sound and pointed. 'Sounds as though he ain't beaten yet, though.'

'Perhaps not, but he can't hold out much longer,' muttered Bart worriedly. He threw swift glances in all directions, trying to pick out a place where they could either bring their own fire to bear most effectively, or where they might be able to get inside the building and give help that way, but without being seen by the gunmen outside.

'You figgering on getting inside to help him,' whispered Guthrie.

'That's right,' Bart said softly. He studied the street in front of him. There was the small, narrow alley which led to the rear of the building, but there would undoubtedly be men watching the back just in case Wheeler made an attempt to escape that way. They were there for the purpose of shooting him down if he tried. Bart's eyes were cold and his jaw set hard as he glanced up at the narrow balcony which ran along the side of the building. If he could get up there without being seen, with Guthrie covering him, there was the chance that he might be able to find a way into the building, or if that failed, he could work his way around to the back and take any of the gunslingers there completely by surprise and off guard. They would be intent watching for anyone trying to sneak out of the back door, without bothering what went on over their heads. The more he thought about it the more feasible it seemed. He explained his plan to Guthrie. The other listened and then nodded quickly. 'I'll cover you from the side, Bart,' he said quietly. 'If you do have to take those men at the back, signal and I'll help.'

Swiftly, Bart made it across the street. Here, in the darkness, it was possible to move without running much risk of being seen. Everyone seemed to be further along the street, outside the editorial office. Even as he reached the other side and lay crouched behind the wooden uprights, Bart heard the shattering of window glass as more fire poured into the office where Ben Wheeler was fighting his last and greatest battle on the side of truth. Grimly, Bart jumped for the bottom of the balcony, felt his fingertips catch on the hard wood, then he began to pull himself up, keeping as silent as he could. The strain on his arms was almost more than he could bear. His body still had not fully recovered from the beating it had taken when those two thugs had tried to kill him on the Clayburne spread. Gritting his teeth, he edged his way up, felt his fingers slip for one moment and braced himself tautly, but with a superhuman effort, he succeeded in retaining his grip and gradually swinging his body up over the low balustrade and on to the balcony. Breathing heavily, he lay there for several moments, sucking air into his lungs, waiting for the weakness in his arms and legs to clear. He could just make out the dark shape that was Guthrie as the other wormed his way forward, keeping his head low, making scarcely any sound.

Very carefully, he edged his way along the balcony. There were no windows here and it was impossible to get in this way. He cursed a little under his breath as he realized that he would have to carry out the second plan and try to take any men at the back by surprise. It only needed one of the men to open fire and give the warning, and the shot could bring most of the men from the street racing around to the rear.

Several horses were tethered below the far end of the balcony, standing quietly in the narrow alley. The sight of them only served to increase the tension in his mind. Blinking his eyes to accustom them to the darkness here, he went on again, an inch at a time, scarcely daring to breathe, his eyes swivelling slowly from side to side as he tried to pick out any faint movement in the shadows down below. For a moment, he paused, then he went to the very edge of the balcony and signalled to Guthrie down below, saw the other lift his left hand in answer, and went on again, sliding the gun from its holster. As he started to edge around the corner of the balcony one of the horses below suddenly skittered and pawed at the ground nervously. Whether or not it had sensed his presence there, it was impossible to tell, but that sudden sound and movement was enough to freeze him in his tracks as he waited for any reaction it might have. For a moment, there was silence down below, then at the corner of Bart's vision, one of the shadows suddenly moved. A man came forward into the open and stood beside the horse.

'What's the matter boy, did you hear something?' The man's voice was gruff and once he glanced up towards the balcony, stepping back a little way to get a better view, eyes narrowed. Bart lay as still as possible, hand on his gun, ready to use it if the man showed the least sign of being suspicious. But after a pause, the other suddenly shook his head and moved away into the darkness again.

Exhaling slowly. Bart pushed himself on to his hands and knees, waited for a moment, listening to the rattle of gunfire from the main street behind him, feeling the urgency within him as he realized that there was only one man inside that office, an old man who knew little of gunplay and yet who had stood up fearlessly against these outlaws. daring to print the truth about them, even though he knew that it would almost inevitably cost him his life.

For a moment, Bart felt the sickening sense of defeat. The people of Cochita City did not seem to have backed their editor when it came to the showdown. He could hear no firing from anywhere else to show that they were coming out on the side of this one man who had dared to show up Zena Clayburne for what she really was, the ruling power behind the outlaws and rustlers, the woman who had given shelter to them, and whose herd now numbered close on ten thousand head, almost all of them taken from the ranchers in the terri-tory and from the men who drove their herds south towards Abilene.

For a moment, as he paused at the corner of the balcony, searching the dimness below him for any sign of the outlaws, he wondered if she was in town, or whether she had decided not to show her face until she was certain that everything had gone in her favour. By now, she would know that Jake and Clem had not succeeded in killing him, that they had been killed themselves and she would have second thoughts about venturing into town, especially now that the townsfolk knew something about her. Not until she had crushed any resistance that might be there, would she show herself and really take over everything.

For a long minute, he crouched there in the cold darkness. He could make out the dark shapes of three men down below him, hugging the wall of the building, their guns in their hands, ready to use them the moment Wheeler appeared through the door at the rear. Bart smiled grimly to himself as he eased his body forward until he was poised over two of the men, crouching close together. The third was some distance away, and he knew that he would have to leave him to Guthrie. He could not take all three of them himself without too much noise. A single shot might be lost in the bedlam of sound that still came from the front of the building. More than that, some of the outlaws were sure to come and investigate the commotion.

Out of the corner of his eye, he saw Guthrie move forward, his body blending well with the shadows. None of the three men had noticed him yet. All of their attention seemed to be concentrated on the door some ten yards away. Carefully, an inch at a time, Bart moved to the very edge of the balcony, threw one leg over the balustrade and hung poised there for several moments, while Guthrie moved up into position. One of the men below moved, easing his body into a more comfortable position. A moment later, Bart dropped from the balcony. His feet caught one of them on the back of the neck, sending him sprawling full length in the dirt. A gush of air escaped from his lips as the blow knocked all of the wind out

of his body. The man next to him tried to turn to meet this
unexpected attack, went reeling back as Bart hit him full in
the face with his bunched fist. He struck his head against the
wall of the building, uttered a low moan and then fell forward.
The first man, pushing himself up on to his hands and knees,
groped blindly for the gun which had fallen from his fingers
and which was lying a few feet away from his outstretched
fingers. Bart leaned forward and placed his foot on the other's
hand, grinding down on it with his heel. The man uttered a
harsh yell of agony, a yell that was cut off a split second later
as Bart laid the barrel of his Colt along his skull. His head
snapped forward and he lay still in the dirt. Lifting his head,
Bart glanced about him, ready to go to Guthrie's help. But the
oldster needed no help. The third man lay slumped against
the wall in one corner and Guthrie was getting slowly to his
feet, glancing down at the rifle in his hands.

'He never knew we were there,' he said proudly. 'Do we go
in now, Bart?'

'Yeah, but be careful. Wheeler is likely to be a trigger-
happy man by now and if we come creeping up on him from
the rear, he's just as likely to shoot us as those polecats
outside. I'd better go first and let him know who we are.'

Quickly, he made his way along the passage and through
the small room at the back with Guthrie close on his heels.
The thunder of gunfire seemed to have reached a sudden
crescendo outside as he opened the door of the room and
stepped through, checking the other's sudden, whirling
movement with a hissed command.

'Hold your fire, Ben. It's me, Bart Shannon. I've brought
along someone to help us hold off those coyotes outside.'

'Glad to have you here, Bart – you too, Guthrie,' nodded
the other. He ducked instinctively, as a fusillade of shots
crashed through the splintered glass of the window. Bullets
hummed through the air and hammered into the wall at the
back of the room as Bart flung himself to the floor. Beside
him, Guthrie crouched down low, his voice hard as he said:

'There must be close on thirty men out there. Bart. How do you figger on keeping them at bay? Pretty soon, we're going to run out of ammunition. Then we won't be able to stop 'em.'

'Then we'll have to make every bullet count, won't we?' Bart's voice was equally grim. He wormed his way forward, reaching the desk placed close to the smashed glass in the front of the office. More slugs whined through the window. Swiftly, he fired back, saw one man on the far side of the street suddenly go up on to his toes as the bullet caught him in the chest. He hung there for a moment as though held up on strings, then crashed down on to his face in the street, his gun flying from his hand. Two other men leapt for shelter behind a trough, crouching down out of sight.

Bart lifted his gun again, then stopped as a harsh, thick voice from the darkness outside yelled: 'Listen to me, Wheeler. You can't hope to hold out for ever. I've got thirty men here and you won't git any help from the townsfolk. They know what'll happen if they try to throw in their lot with you. Come on out of there with your hands over your head. We only want to talk to you.'

'Nothing doing, Saunders,' Wheeler called back. 'I don't aim to let you shoot me in the back like you did Sheriff Keene.'

There was a moment's silence from outside, then the voice came again: 'This is your last warning, Wheeler. We don't know where you dug up that information about Miss Clayburne and me, but you know that it was all lies. Print that tomorrow and nothing will happen. If you don't accept this offer, we'll rush you and smash everything there, after we've strung you up.'

'That's what I figure you'll do whether I come out and give myself up or not.' Wheeler fired a couple of shots in the direction of the voice, but they had no effect for Saunders called a moment later. 'If that's your answer, that's the way you'll get it.'

127

Gunfire started up again from the whole length of the street facing the office. Bart crouched lower as bullets droned over his head like a cloud of angry hornets. A ricochet screamed thinly as it struck the press and whined around the room. Lunging forward, he reached the edge of the window, knocked a sliver of glass away with the end of the gun barrel and fired a couple of shots at two men who ran from cover behind a barrel on the far side of the street, trying to make their way over to the other side, to get in close.

The first man doubled over as if hit in the solar plexus by a savage blow. For a moment, he stood there, bent in the middle, then he fell forward against the legs of the other man, throwing him off balance. Bart's second shot passed through the air where the other man's head had been a moment earlier. His third shot, the Colt bucking savagely against his wrist, did not miss. The man went down with a wild cry and lay still in the middle of the street. That ought to give Saunders something to think about, he thought grimly. By now, the other would be wondering where all of the fire was coming from. As far as Saunders knew, he was dead and there was no one else in the town who would dare to help Wheeler.

A bullet ploughed into the wood close to Bart's head and he flinched drawing back instinctively. For a moment, he failed to see where it had come from, then he noticed the sudden sharp flicker of movement out of the corner of his eye, saw the man crouched on the balcony of the building opposite, a man with a rifle which was slowly being brought to bear on him again. Down and up, Bart lifted the long barrel of the Colt in a sweeping motion that tilted the gun muzzle an inch above the distant target. A single swift snap of the wrist and the sights came to bear. Squeezing the trigger, he felt the weapon buck and kick as sound hammered in his ear. The man's shoulders rocked as the bullet found its mark. He fell forward, slumped for an instant against the guard rail. What happened next was so swift that it was impossible afterward for Bart to say whether the rail was rotten, or whether the other's weight, thrown so violently against it, had caused it to snap. But it broke away from him, tilting outwards over the street as he slumped forward, the wood splintering. The sound of the man's scream was an eerie wail that echoed along the street, even above the sound of gunfire. It sent a little shiver along Bart's veins as he watched the man drop like a stone, his body bouncing a little as it struck the dirt beneath the balcony. Neck broken by the shuddering impact, the man lay still and behind him, the other outlaws continued to fire over his still body as if it never existed.

Bart sucked in a deep breath. Searching with eyes and ears, he tried to locate the position of Jeb Saunders. Once that man was killed, he felt convinced that the others would soon break off the battle. He was the guiding force behind this attack. He it was who held them together, the man they feared above anyone else, except for Zena Clayburne. But wherever Saunders was, he seemed intent on remaining under cover. He could have been any one of the dark shapes that were visible at intervals as they lifted their bodies to enable them to fire into the office, through the shattered panes of glass. In the faint light that filtered into the room from the saloon across the street, the splinters of glass which covered the floor glittered like a pile of diamonds. Bart forced himself to look away and concentrate on what was happening over the street. There were still twenty-five men left and his own stock of ammunition was running low. He doubted if they could hold out until dawn and it would be several hours after sun-up before the troops could get there. If only he had known about those papers earlier, and he could have sent proof of Zena Clayburne's complicity in the rustlings earlier to the Fort, all of this might have been avoided by now. He tightened his lips, clenching his teeth in his head until they hurt. There was a dull ache suffused throughout the whole of his body now, muscles and nerves that protested against the beating they had taken over the past few days. A man could drive himself so far, and no further, he reflected. After that, something had to give and he knew that he was almost at the limit of his endurance. Another bullet ploughed into the wood less than an inch from his head and he cursed himself for neglecting to keep his attention on the street. At the very edge of his vision, he saw that a small bunch of men who had worked their way further along the street, so as to be out of range of their guns, were rushing across to the nearer side, ready to work their way along the fronts of the wooden buildings, until they could get within range again. Attacked from two sides like that, things would be almost hopeless for the three of them.

He narrowed his eyes and did some fast thinking. It was impossible to say whether Saunders had sent any more men around to the back of the building to check on what was happening there. If he had, then they might be getting ready to move into the back of the building, might even at that moment be working their way along the narrow passage and into the room at the other side of that closed door. Carefully, he edged his way back from the window. Bullets struck the floor on either side of his legs as he leapt for shelter behind the desk. He crouched low beside Guthrie. 'Think you can hold them off for a while? I want to take a look see at the back. I've a feeling Saunders may have sent some of his men to the rear to check up on the others and if he has, it would-n't surprise me if they aren't working their way up on us at this very moment.'

'Sure thing, Bart.' The other nodded, snapped a quick shot at a running figure that showed for an instant against the light from the saloon windows. Bart threw a quick glance into the street and grinned faintly to himself. There was still noth-ing wrong with the old man's aim, he realized. The figure now lay sprawled in the dirt, arms outflung, legs twisted beneath him.

'Keep it up like that and we'll come through,' he whis-pered. 'Try not to waste any ammunition. And watch out for some men on this side of the street. They're out there now, trying to work their way along the fronts of the buildings. If they get within shooting distance, shoot.'

He wormed his way to the back of the room, past the huge metal shape of the press. A couple of slugs whined screechingly off the tough metal and ploughed deep furrows in the wall beyond. Reaching the door, Bart eased it open, paused for a moment, then slipped through into the room. For a moment, he fought to adjust his eyes to the darkness here. Even after the faint light in the front room, it was difficult to make out anything here and he knew that he had made a perfect target for any gunman who might happen to be there, the moment he had slipped through the door and shown himself against the patch of light. But there was no ominous click of a hammer being drawn back and an instant later, he was on the other side of the room, staring along the narrow passage that stretched away to the back of the building. He felt a sense of relief wash through him as he noticed that it was empty. He was on the point of turning back to rejoin the others when something moved at the far end and he caught a fragmentary glimpse of the burly figure of one of the gunslingers moving in through the open door. Swiftly, he pressed his body back against the wall and waited. There were at least two more out there, he told himself fiercely and he wanted to get all of them in his sights before he opened fire. The second man stepped into view behind the first, the faint light glinting off the barrel of the gun he carried in his right hand. His face was in shadow, but Bart did not doubt that these were two of the men he and Guthrie had slugged earlier. It had not taken them long to come round. The men were halfway along the passage now, wary and cautious. It seemed impossible that they could be so close and yet could not see him as he waited in the darkness at the far end. But the light was at the back of them, showing up their figures quite plainly even in the dimness, whereas he had darkness at his back and there was nothing to make his body stand out.

He waited tensely for the third man to put in an appear-

ance. It was just possible that he had been sent back to warn
Saunders of what had happened and Bart was on the point of
lifting the gun to cut down the two men when the last man
showed briefly at their backs. He was more wary than the
others. He hung back, evidently deciding that if there was
going to be trouble, and he probably had a sixth sense that
told him there would be, he wanted to be in a position to get
out with an even chance of escape. Something inside Bart
took over control of his hand, the hand which held the gun.
It was something that had been rising ever since they had
pulled out of the Guthrie place, leaving it behind them in the
darkness, a smouldering ruin, with Jason's grave to keep it
company. A tightening anger that threatened to take over
complete control of his mind. Almost of its own volition, his
finger squeezed on the trigger, squeezed three times, the gun
tilting a fraction of an inch after every shot. The first two men
stumbled forward as the bullets bit deeply into their bodies.
One of them managed to live long enough to loose off a
single shot, but it was a purely involuntary action, a squeezing
of the trigger by a finger convulsed in death and the bullet
struck the floor of the passage several feet in front of Bart.
The third man was already turning when the shot hit him. It
struck him in the fleshy part of the shoulder and went deep.
He let out a savage bellow of pain and caught at the side of
the passage as he pulled himself up straight and thrust his
feet out in front of him, forcing them to move, to get him out
of danger. He seemed to be walking forward drunkenly, as
though his legs were encased in lead and his body, turned
fully with its back to Bart, was outlined perfectly against the
dim light. This kind of killing was not normally in Bart, shooting a man in the back as he tried to get away, but that little
voice at the back of his mind told him that this was one of the
outlaws who had killed his companions on the bank of the
river all those long, weary days ago and he deserved no better
death. Only for the briefest fraction of a second did his finger
hesitate on the trigger. Then he squeezed it and saw the other

stagger once more as the slug tore into his back, thrusting him forward on to his knees. He collapsed in the entrance to the passage and lay still, a hump of unmoving shadow.

Without pausing, Bart ran forward, jumping over the still bodies of the men he had just killed, until he reached the door. Carefully, he edged out into the yard at the back and peered about him, looking for any other men who might have been holed up there, ready to cut off their escape if things got too hot for them in the front. The yard seemed deserted. If there was anyone there, he was keeping himself well hidden and did not intend to give his hiding place away. Possibly, he had seen what had happened to his three companions and did not want to share the same fate at the hands of this fast gunman.

He remained there only a few moments longer, then went back into the office. Guthrie threw him a swift glance as he came in. Gunfire continued to crash and echo along the length of the street.

'Anything happening out there?' he asked tightly. 'I caught three *hombres* trying to sneak in the back way. Must have been those three we laid out when we came in. They're dead now.'

'There seems to be a bunch of critters moving up from the right, close to the front of the building,' murmured Ben hoarsely. 'Can't quite make out what they're up to, but I don't like it. They wouldn't get that close unless they intended to do something. They can't bring their guns to bear on us in here without exposing themselves too much, so I don't reckon they're there just for that.'

'Keep me covered while I take a look,' muttered Bart. Keeping his head low, he scuttled across the floor to the edge of the window, his feet crunching in the framents of glass that littered the floor. Going down on one knee, he threw a swift glance along the street. At first, he could see nothing, then he made out the small group of men, clustered together some ten yards from the front of the office. Screwing up his eyes, he tried to make out what they were doing. They had dragged something with them, something he could not identify because two of them were squatting in front of it. He threw a couple of shots in their direction, hoping to make them move, but the slugs ricocheted off the wall and went screaming over their heads. Almost as if it had been a pre-arranged signal, the two shots brought an avalanche of fire from the opposite side of the street. Every gun seemed to have opened up on them and the reason was obvious: to force them to keep their heads down while that small group of men advanced.

The men edged closer. Still it was impossible to see the reason behind this move. It was unlikely that men would risk their lives for nothing. Then he saw why they were there. A sudden flare of light, a burst of yellow-and-red edged flame and the bale of straw which the men had been pulling along the boardwalk was blazing furiously. He guessed, from the way it burned, that it had been soaked in paraffin. Thrusting at it with a couple of long poles, the men sent it careering along the boardwalk until it came to rest against the dry timber of the wall. The flames began to leap hungrily up the side. Like tinder, the wood caught instantly.

Swiftly, he ran back into the room, ignoring the bullets that hummed about him and plucked at the sleeve of his jacket. 'Get some water,' he yelled, grabbing Wheeler by the arm. 'They're trying to burn us out.'

Ben Wheeler had already seen the danger, for he pushed himself to his feet and ran to the far corner of the room. When he came back, he was carrying a heavy stone jar in his hands. Bart looked at him in amazement for a moment.

'Is that water?' he asked thickly.

Ben shook his head as he brushed past him. A moment later and he was at the wall, the flames licking up about him. Scorning them, ignoring the bullets that flailed the air, he up-ended the jar and a stream of black liquid poured on to the flames with a hissing sound. A second fled before Bart realized what it was that he was using so effectively. Then he knew: printers' ink. But it was not flowing fast enough through the narrow neck of the jar to put out the fire in time, Bart realized, and glanced about him for something else. The next second, Wheeler had staggered back a couple of inches and there was the shattering sound of stone being smashed. A bullet had struck the jar in the very centre, smashing it to shards, emptying the contents on to the flames in a single, rushing torrent.

On the other side of the street, the outlaws re-doubled their fire and before Bart could shout a warning to the other, Wheeler staggered and fell against the wall, clutching at his shoulder as he fell. In a couple of strides, Bart was beside him, pulling at the shirt, trying to locate the wound. It was fairly high in the fleshy part and looked more dangerous than it really was. But it meant that he would be unable to use a gun and there were now only two of them against Jeb Saunders and the other gunslammers from the Clayburne spread.

'Get back under cover,' he said urgently to the other. 'Guthrie and I will try to hold them off.'

'You don't have a chance,' muttered Ben dispiritedly. 'We're finished now. Why don't you try to get out through the back. This is not your fight, Bart. You've got no stake in this town, Why don't you let it go on down the trail to ruin if that's what the people want. They've had their chance to fight for a decent way of life, freedom from fear, from the gunshot in the night, from ranches that are burned down in reprisal. I've told them the truth and still they either don't believe, or they're too scared to do anything about it.' He sighed as the other took him by the good arm and led him back into the room.

'After tonight, I'm convinced that Sheriff Keene died in vain. He tried to fight for law and order and all he got for his pains was a bullet in the back.' He drew in a deep breath as a spasm of pain passed through him. 'That isn't the right way for a man to die, not a fighting man like he was. They were

135

afraid to go gunning for him face to face, so they had to take the coward's way out.'

'Just you sit there and keep your head down,' said Bart smoothly. 'It'll be dawn in a little while and if we can hold out until then, we may be safe.'

The other shrugged, but said nothing. Bart went back to the desk in front of the window and rejoined Guthrie. 'Still no let up in their fire, Bart,' said the other quietly. There was no fear, no trace of defeat in his voice. Just a calm acceptance of the facts. 'And we're almost clean out of ammunition. Another twenty shells left and then it's the end. I wonder if they know how short we are?'

'If they don't, they soon will,' said Bart grimly, 'If we only had something else with which to fight them.'

'There'll only be our bare hands once we've used all of our slugs.'

Bart rubbed the haze from his eyes, reloaded the guns in his hands, spun the chambers, then waited for a target to show itself. There was a faint grey light just visible outside now as the dawn began to brighten in the east. By now, Tess ought to have reached Fort Apache with his message to the colonel. If he acted on it immediately as he guessed he would provided he had the men to spare, they ought to be in Cochita City by about noon, if they rode hard. He had delib-erately imparted a tone of urgency to the message, although at the time he had written it, he had not guessed just how urgent the position would really be.

'They're trying to move in on us, Bart,' gritted the other tightly.

Bart lifted his head and peered across the street. Several men had risen from behind the barrels where they had hidden themselves and were rushing forward, covered by the others in the saloon, shooting through the windows.

'Wait until I give the word, then make every shot count,' said Bart grimly, The tightness in his chest was almost intol-erable now. Now the gunslingers were facing them. Bart let his eyes run over the men who came forward. In the grey light that washed over them, their faces were tight, drawn into masks which showed no expression. They could not know how many men were in the office, facing them, possibly they figured that they had killed Wheeler and they had only to walk in and take over the place. Bart's cold grey eyes held steadily on the line of advancing men. Bullets still flew over his head as he crouched down and the breath felt raw and cold in his lungs and throat. But he held his fire, finger tight on the trigger, knowing that Guthrie would do likewise until he gave the order.

'Now,' he hissed sharply. Both guns bucked and jerked in his hands as he loosed off rapid shots. The men in the street faltered. Evidently they had not expected to meet sustained and accurate fire such as this. Saunders had probably told them that there was nothing more to fear from whoever was in the office, that they were either out of ammunition or killed. Five men fell as the withering, scything hail of fire swept across them. The others hesitated for a moment, firing wild, then broke, turned and ran back under cover.

Bart could just make out Saunders yelling something harshly at them and once more he tried to locate the other. Then he saw him, the black-bearded face unmistakable, at the end of the boardwalk on the far side of the street. He snapped a quick shot at Saunders, saw the face vanish instantly so that it was impossible to tell whether his shot had found its target.

Moments later, Saunders yelled. 'All right, Shannon. We know that you're in there with Wheeler. Reckon that we can bide our time. We've got plenty of food and water out here. Reckon you've got none in there and it's going to be a hot day.' There was a savage bellow of sarcastic laughter.

Bart leaned back against the desk and slipped his last remaining shells into the guns. His belt was now empty. Once the Colts were empty, that was the finish as far as he was concerned.

The gunfire died away and there was silence in the street of Cochita City. The citizens, sensing that there was death in the air, had withdrawn to each end of the street, making no move to come into the fight. With an effort, Bart pushed himself up on to his feet and went back into the middle of the room. He examined Wheeler's wound once more. There was a purpling of the flesh around the ragged hole but the bleeding had stopped. The lead was still inside him somewhere but he hesitated to probe for it. The other was still pretty weak and he had no proper implements for that, no boiling water. He doubted if the other could have taken anything like that.

'How's it feeling?' be asked softly.

'Just numb now,' replied the other, pulling his lips back into a travesty of a smile. 'It's still in there, isn't it?'

'Afraid so. I'd like to take it out, but I don't think it would be wise at the moment. We've very little water here and what we have, we'll need for drinking.'

The other licked his lips. He turned his head slightly to look in the direction of the street. 'What's happened out there?' he inquired hoarsely. 'They've stopped firing. Don't tell me that you managed to drive them off?'

Bart shook his head slowly. 'Nothing like that,' he said grimly. 'They've just decided there's no sense in losing any more men. They're going to sit it out, hoping that we'll soon be forced to go out when our water runs out.'

'There isn't much water here,' acknowledged the other dully. 'And no more ammunition.'

'Just you lie back and rest,' murmured Bart softly. 'Leave me to do the worrying. If we can hold on, the troops ought to be here soon.'

CHAPTER VII

RANGE WAR

The sun was a glaring sickening disc in the cloudly white sky. It threw long beams of gold into the room where the three men lay, lit the splinters of glass with fiery gleams until they shone brilliantly and hurt the eyes to look at them. Outside, in the dusty street, other men waited in silence behind barrels and water troughs, behind the broken windows of the saloon. Hard-eyed men whose orders were to slay and kill those three men in the building opposite.

Bart Shannon shifted his legs for what seemed the hundredth time in a vain effort to ease the stabbing, lancing pains of cramp that shot through the muscles of his legs. Sweat formed continually on his forehead and laced down the ridges and folds of skin on his cheeks, running into his eyes and half blinding him. Inside the room, the heat was almost intolerable. Dust drifted in through the shattered holes in the window, went down into his lungs until they burned like fire with every breath that he took.

Beside him, Guthrie lay full length on the floor, the rifle beside him. His eyes were half closed, but he was not asleep. There could be no sleep for them until the troops arrived in Cochita City, or they died at the hands of the outlaws who were waiting for them to make a move. Bart swallowed thickly

139

and forced himself to think clearly. Judging from the shadows in the street, the sun was almost at its zenith. Soon it would be high noon. If the soldiers did not come then, they might still be forced to shoot it out with their last bullets and go down fighting. And what of the people of the town? The men who carried guns but were afraid to use them. They had seen for themselves that these outlaws could be killed, that they were not supermen. And yet they had refused to join in and help the three men who were fighting so that law and order might be brought back to the town.

Bart checked the slugs in the chambers of his guns. Ten left. Ten bullets to take care of more than twenty men. He doubted whether Guthrie would have as many. And there were none left in Wheeler's gun.

'Any sign of movement out there?' asked Wheeler. He pushed himself up on to his side, wincing with pain as he moved. 'It seems mighty quiet in the street.'

'They're still biding their time,' muttered Bart thinly. 'Sooner or later, they have to make a move. When they do, I figure they'll try to rush us. They must know by now that we can't have much ammunition left.'

'And the townsfolk. Still at the end of the street, looking on?' There was a note of disgust in the other's tone. 'I'm beginning to be real sorry that I went to the trouble of printing that paper yesterday. I thought it might help to rouse them. I reckon I could have saved my time. When Zena Clayburne takes over the whole town, they'll wonder why they allowed it to happen, but by that time, it'll be too late for them to do anything about it.'

Bart nodded slowly. Waves of heat shocked off the street outside, making the details of the building opposite shimmer in front of his eyes.

It was high noon in Cochita City. There was a pall-like silence hanging over everything, a silence like that of the grave, crowding down over everything. Tension seemed to crackle

140

on the still air like a distant storm brewing on the horizon, ready to break at any moment. It was as if it needed only the slightest sound to start the gunfire all over again. Slowly, wearily, Bart shook his head. Had something happened to Tess on the way to Fort Apache? It was something that could not be dismissed entirely. There was always the possibility that Zena Clayburne had been too smart for them, that she had had men watching that trail just on the chance that he might try to send for help. He bit his lower lip at the idea and tried to thrust it into the background of his mind, to forget about it for the time being, knowing that thoughts such as that only served to slow a man's reflexes when the time came for battle.

Guthrie wiped the sweat from his face with the back of his sleeve and moved his legs slowly. 'How much longer are they going to be before they decide to do something?' he muttered. Tension gave an odd edge to his voice and there was a queer look at the back of his eyes. He was worried about his daughter. Bart could see that in his face, although the other was trying desperately not to show it.

Bart's hands were rigid, clenched tightly around the guns. He seemed to have been lying there, waiting for something to happen for an eternity. When it did happen, it came with the shock of the unexpected. A man flashed into sight on the boardwalk in front of the saloon. In the same second another appeared at one of the windows. A split second later, the street rocked and bucketed with gunfire. Savagely, Bart pulled his head down, cursing. Bullets hummed through the air close to his body, hammering into the desk which had been up-ended in front of the window to provide them with a little cover. Two men with rifles had taken up their positions on the veranda over the boardwalk and were firing down into the room, choosing their targets carefully.

Bart lay rigid and waited. He had no ammunition to waste and was determined to pick his targets when there was little chance of missing. At the corner of the street, where one of the alleys intersected the main street, he caught a glimpse of

141

Saunders. The tall, black-bearded man was out of range of their guns and he did not waste time or precious ammunition firing at him. All of the hate within him boiled up anew at the sight of Saunders.

The crash of gunfire rose to a savage crescendo. Bart toppled one of the men off the veranda, then paused as an amazing change came over the scene. For a moment it was impossible for him to take it in. From somewhere out of sight, there came the sound of gunfire, matching that of the outlaws, gunfire that sent several of the gunslingers toppling into the street. Taken utterly by surprise, the men turned and fled, leaving more than half of their number dead in the street. Bart found himself staring with amazement at the scene in front of him, then aware that the battle was over, he lowered the guns in his hands, and thrust them deep into the holsters, knowing with a strange certainty that they would not be needed again.

Somewhere in the distance, there rose the strangely haunting sound of a bugle, a sound that carried easily in the silence. Guthrie climbed to his feet and let out a war-whoop as he ran for the door. Throwing it open, he stepped out into the street. Bart followed close on his heels. The troops came riding along the main street, their horses throwing up a cloud of dry dust that settled only slowly in the sunlight. Bart went forward as the man in the lead reined his horse and sat in the saddle looking down at him.

'Glad you came when you did, Colonel,' he said warmly, taking the other's hand. 'We were almost finished in there. Ben Wheeler, the town editor, has a bullet in the shoulder but I reckon he ought to be fine once the doctor takes a look at it.'

'We were glad to be of assistance,' smiled the other. He eyed Bart shrewdly. 'I must admit I was a little surprised when I got your note just before dawn. Isn't this a new kind of business for you'? I always thought you were a cattle man. Yet here I find you trying to take over a town.'

Bart nodded. 'Those men bushwhacked the herd we were driving to Abilene some days ago. I was the only survivor. Dodson was killed but before he died, I swore I'd hunt down his killers and see that they paid for what they did. They're all in the pay of Zena Clayburne.' He looked about him as another thought struck him. The troops had moved out and were heading after the outlaws, many of whom were trying to make their get-away.

The colonel caught the direction of his glance and guessed at the thought behind it. 'Don't worry about them,' he said quietly. 'My men will round them up. I reckon we have enough evidence against all of them to bring them to trial. As for Zena Clayburne, I think we'd better take a ride out to her ranch for a little talk.'

'Could be that you'll find the bird has flown,' said Bart quickly. His keen gaze sought for some sign of Jeb Saunders, but he had vanished. By now, Bart reflected, the gunman would be riding hell for leather to warn Zena Clayburne that their gamble had failed, that the troops were in Cochita City and their empire was rapidly falling in ruins about their ears. 'The leader of those men will be on his way back to the ranch by now. I've got to stop him.'

Before the other could say anything, Bart was running back along the street to where his mount was still tethered. Without breaking stride, he leapt into the saddle, rode back quickly to where the colonel sat.

'I'll need ammunition,' he said quickly, urgently.

The other did not hesitate. As if he sensed that this was something between the gunhawk and Bart, he handed over his own belt, watched closely while Bart buckled it on, then said quickly. 'I'll take my men out to the Clayburne spread. We'll meet you there.'

Bart did not wait to reply. Kicking spurs to the sorrel, he felt the magnificent animal leap forward, throwing up the dust of the street under its hoofs as he rode swiftly out of town. By now, Saunders would have a good start on him, but he was guessing that he would stick to the trail which led through the valley. He intended to swing further north, into the timber line, cutting over the hills, taking a trail which ought to intersect Saunders less than two miles from the boundary fence of the Clayburne ranch. Pressing on, he followed the main trail for half a mile, keeping his eyes on it, watching for the tell-tale prints which would indicate that a rider had passed that way only a little time before, riding his mount hard. To the north of the town, the nature of the country did not favour him. Although open, it was an undulating succession of low hills, with little open space for him to be able to pick out the man he pursued. A mile further on, he swung off the trail, set his mount into the rocks. Every muscle and fibre within him screamed for action now, but he held himself under tight control. Saunders was still a dangerous man. He had deliberately kept himself in the background during the gunfight in the town, not through fear, but because he was a shrewd fighter, in spite of his reputation as a fast gun and there were bigger things at stake here than meeting Bart Shannon face to face.

A while later, Bart entered the timber country on the crest of the low range of hills which lay to the south of the Clayburne range. Here, the trail wound in and out of the trees, making it difficult for him to push the horse as much as he would have liked. There were moments when he found himself doubting the wisdom of coming in this direction. In his mind's eye, he could visualize Saunders drawing still further ahead, the outlaw's horse as fresh as his own. When he finally came out of the timber, looking down over the plain which lay beyond, he could see no sign of him at first as he slitted his eyes against the flooding glare of the lowering sun. Then he caught the flicker of movement, turned his head quickly and picked out the figure of the solitary rider, moving quickly in a cloud of dust along the trail below. Saunders had made better time than he had thought possible. Swiftly, he raked the rowel of the spurs across the sorrel's flanks, putting it down the rocky trail. Sure-footed, the animal raced down the steep slope. One wrong move would have sent both horse and rider hurtling down the steep trail, possibly to their death, but Bart thought nothing of this as he kept his eye on the rider below him, judging his speed nicely. He reached the trail where it ran behind tall rocks and reined the sorrel. The faint sound of the approaching horse reached him a moment later. He waited until Saunders rounded the sharply-angled bend in the trail, then rode out in front of him. Saunders's mount reared up in sudden alarm and he fought for control, his face a tight mask. An expert horseman, his hands were already flashing for the guns at his waist, before the horse had settled its feet on the ground. His draw was quick, almost too fast to be seen with the eye, but fast as it was, Bart's was quicker. The guns seemed to leap into his hands, lining up on the other, his fingers squeezing the triggers so that the two shots sounded like one. Saunders succeeded in firing one shot before the two slugs took him in the chest. Bart felt the slug burn a line along his left arm and for a moment, his hand went numb. Stiffly upright in the saddle, he rode forward as the other toppled forward, sliding sideways on to the hard rocks. He fell heavily, the guns slipping from his fingers. Sliding from his own saddle, Bart went forward, going down on one knee beside the other. Saunders tried to pull himself up on to his hands, but the effort was too much for him. With a bubbling cough, he fell back, his eyes wide open, a leering sneer on his lips.

'I had you figured for dead, Shannon,' he said thickly. His lips moved and he tried to swallow. 'I never figured you would come riding after me.'

'I reckoned you'd try to warn Zena Clayburne what had happened in town,' said Bart harshly. 'She's got to pay the penalty for what she's done, just as you have. I always swore that I'd kill you for what you did when you bushwhacked that herd. Now the score's evened.'

'And you reckon that you're going to take Miss Clayburne

in?' A faint smile touched the other's lips and for a moment his eyes cleared. He said distinctly: 'Reckon there's something you ought to know about Zena, Shannon. You've got her figured for a hard and ruthless woman. But she's more than that – a lot more. I've known her for a long time now, I know what she's really like.' He paused, moved his lips for a moment, then fell into a paroxysm of coughing. Bart eased the other's head up from the hard rocks. All of the hatred for this man seemed to have burned itself out inside him.

He waited for Saunders to go on, knowing that the man was dying, that only something deep within him, some strange driving force kept him alive until he got something off his chest. For a moment, the other's lips moved, but no words came out. Then, when he did speak, his voice was almost a whisper so that Bart had to lean forward to hear what he said.

'She's a she-devil, Shannon. I ought to know. I've seen what she's done to men who tried to face up to her. There was a Pinkerton man too. He came snooping around on the spread. She took that whip of hers to him. When she'd finished with him, he was crying out for death. It would have been more human to have shot him down the minute he showed his face.'

'There's no need to worry on that score,' said Bart evenly. 'She's going to get all that's coming to her. Now that the troops have moved in to bring a little law and order to the place, I reckon the townsfolk might lose their fear of her and take things into their own hands. If they do, then God help Zena Clayburne.'

The other was silent for a long moment, so quiet that Bart glanced down at him, thinking that he had died. But Saunders's eyes were still fixed on him with a hard, bright stare and after a moment, he said thinly: 'You got those papers out of Jason's safe?'

Bart gave a quick nod. 'They named you as the man who shot Sheriff Keene in the back,' he said tonelessly.

'I know.' A pause, then: 'Have you ever wondered why they weren't destroyed? Why Zena Clayburne insisted that Jason should keep them there?'

Bart nodded again. 'Some warped sense of humour,' he muttered. 'Can't see no other reason for it. Some of those documents can be used against her, those title deeds to that range are illegal.'

'So are those papers about me, Shannon.' The other had difficulty in speaking now. He was forced to pause between every word and the red stain on the front of his shirt widened every second as his life ebbed away with his blood. 'I didn't shoot Keene. Sure I've killed men in my time, but I always faced up to them when I did.'

'Then why—?' Bart paused as the realization came to him in that moment. One look at the other's face confirmed it, even before he got the words out.

'She killed him, Shannon. You've got to believe that. She was there, in the street when it happened. She had a derringer and when he came out of the saloon, she shot him in the back. He never had a chance. But she had to make certain that I never got any ideas about riding out at any time, so she got Jason and a crooked lawyer together and they drew up those papers, brought in a few of the townsfolk to swear that they saw me shoot him down. They didn't have any difficulty doing that. The people were only too willing to swear that they saw me do it. Reckon they liked the old guy and they didn't like professional killers like me, especially as I worked for her.'

'So that's it,' Bart nodded. A lot of little things that had been puzzling him suddenly fell into place. He looked down at the other, saw the sudden change in the mask, the gleam of fierce satisfaction that flitted over the other's pallid features. Then the other fell back against the rocks, his body still.

Slowly, Bart climbed into the saddle. He turned the sorrel's head in the direction of the Clayburne spread. There

147

was another score he had to settle now, before he was finished with killing. He rode slowly now, taking his time, feeling the hatred build up within him afresh. Behind him, somewhere on the trail, were the troops, moving in on Zena Clayburne. But he had too long a start on them to worry about them overtaking him.

At the boundary fence, he found the gap in the wire and rode through. Warily, he watched the trail as he headed for the ranch. Not all of Zena's hired killers would have been in town during the night. There would be others left here in case of further trouble. He topped the low rise a while later and sat for a moment, eyeing the trail behind him. There was a small cloud of dust in the distance and he watched it for a moment with a feeling of satisfaction. The troops riding in on his heels. He estimated that it would take them the best part of half an hour before they arrived at the ranch. Turning back to peer down into the wide valley, he noticed that there were still almost a hundred head of cattle in the stockade.

Everything seemed quiet and peaceful down there and he felt a sense of relief as he realized that his greatest fear had been unfounded; that no one had ridden in ahead of Saunders to warn them at the ranch of what had happened. Almost of their own volition, his hands unloosened the guns in their holsters. He ran a dry tongue over equally dry lips. This, he realized, was the final showdown. The empire which Zena Clayburne had built up on fear and avarice was on the point of being destroyed and he could only hope that when it was finished, something new and better would rise to take its place. There was a big future for Cochita City. It lay at the junction of the two great cattle trails, and in addition, there was good arable land a little to the north where they could grow wheat and grain. Soon, the planners would come and start to build a real city here. The town would grow beyond all imagining, but this would only come if there could be law and order here. If evil prevailed, then there would be no advancement. The herding trail might continue to be there, but they would be by-passed while other towns further north and west grew at their expense.

He was a cattle man himself. He could look ahead to the time when there would be a railroad running through here linking the oldness of the east with the vital newness of the west. There were vast new tracts of land just on the point of being opened up out there, just beyond the horizon. It would be up to the citizens of the town to decide whether they were to share in the wealth and expansion this would bring or not. The choice was theirs.

For a long time, he waited there, sitting motionless in the saddle, keeping a watch on what went on below him. The tightness in his mind did not go away. Through the long days and nights since Dodson and his other companions had been killed, he had dreamed of this day. There had been moments when it seemed that it would never come, when it seemed that the end of Bart Shannon would come first. Now, after all that time, he was here. He was still there when the troops arrived. The colonel gave him a strange glance as he rode up to him, sat beside him for a long moment. Then he said softly: 'We found Saunders back there a piece, Bart. I see you finally caught up with him. Now there's just Zena Clayburne and the remaining killers to take care of.'

'Before you ride in there,' said Bart slowly, 'There's one thing you ought to know. Saunders talked before he died. He talked about Zena Clayburne and of the day when Sheriff Keene was shot down in the back.'

'I remember the incident,' acknowledged the other gravely. 'It was Saunders who did it, but they never convicted him. The jury found him not guilty.'

'I know.' Bart's mouth was tight with a grim amusement. 'It was a rigged jury, but on that particular occasion they were right in their verdict.'

'I'm afraid I don't follow you.' There was a trace of puzzlement on the other's bluff features. 'Are you trying to tell me that he didn't fire that shot?'

'That's right. He had to take the blame because it was all arranged between Zena and some crooked lawyer they had in town. She was the one who killed the sheriff. But she had to put the blame on Saunders, not only to divert it from herself, but also to make certain that she had a sufficient hold on him to keep him there, to ensure that he would obey every little whim of hers. I think you'll find that she killed the Pinkerton agent a while back.'

'I see. And you feel that Saunders was telling the truth.'

'He didn't have anything to lose,' Bart pointed out. 'I know he probably wanted to see that she didn't get off scott free when he was dying. But he was riding here to warn her.'

'Was he, though?' The other's voice was deadly quiet. 'It struck me back there after we had found him, that he might have had another motive for coming here ahead of us. He might have been riding here to kill her. He knew it would all be finished for him, that he couldn't hope to get out of the territory. There's a price on his head in virtually every State. Only here on the Clayburne ranch was he safe from the law. He probably wanted to even an old score with Zena Clayburne before he died.'

Bart nodded slowly. That was something he had not considered, but the more he looked at it, the more feasible it seemed. He doubted if it altered the fact that it had been Zena who had shot Keene. All of the available evidence pointed conclusively to that.

The colonel stirred in the saddle and threw a swift glance in the direction of the ranch, brows puckered in thought. 'Those steers down there in the stockade,' he began, pointing. 'Could they be part of that herd you were bringing through?'

'It's possible. There were four thousand head in our herd. It would take them some little time to alter all of those brands.'

'Then I suggest we ride down now and take a look see.' The other's voice was grim and determined. He turned in his saddle and waved the troopers forward. They were at the bottom of the ridge and almost into the courtyard before they were seen. Bart saw one of the men suddenly glance up, throw them a startled look, then vanish into the ranch. The others hesitated for a moment, then followed him.

'Looks like we're in for trouble,' said the colonel quietly. His voice was flat and toneless. 'If that's the way they want it.'

Almost as if in answer to his quietly spoken words, a rifle barked from one of the windows of the ranch and the bullet ploughed a neat furrow into the earth a few feet in front of Bart's mount. It shied a little, then quietened as it felt his hands on the reins.

'That's far enough, soldier,' called a harsh, feminine voice which Bart recognized instantly as belonging to Zena Clayburne. 'This is private land and you're trespassing on it. I'm giving you a minute to ride off it, otherwise I'll order my men to open fire.'

'Zena Clayburne,' called the colonel loudly. He sat quite still in the saddle and not even a single muscle of his face moved.

'That's right. Now ride on.'

Bart rode forward a couple of yards. 'This is the end of the trail for you, Zena,' he called thinly. 'Your little plan to kill Ben Wheeler didn't succeed. We're here to see that you stand trial.'

'Trial!' There was naked scorn in her voice. 'You're not taking me in on any charge.' The rifle barked again and Bart felt the wind of the bullet as it scorched past his cheek. He pulled his mount back again until he was in line with the others. 'You've got nothing against me.'

'On the contrary,' Bart raised his voice again. 'Saunders talked before he died. We know now that you were the one who shot Sheriff Keene in the back. We also have the documents that you kept in Sheriff Jason's safe. The title deeds to this land aren't worth the paper they're written on. Now this is your last warning, are you coming out peaceably, or do we have to come in and get you?'

'Damn you, Shannon. I ought to have killed you myself when I had the chance!' There was anger in her voice. Seconds later, a fusillade of shots rang out from the windows of the ranch. The colonel ordered his men back, out of range. His face was grim and Bart saw the old, familiar battle-light in his eyes.

He gave his orders quickly, the men scattering as they moved in a large circle around the buildings at the head of the valley. Even Bart was filled with admiration at the way they moved, going forward with a quiet precision. They kept their heads low as more gunfire came from the long, low buildings. Slipping from the saddle, Bart moved forward with the others. Running with his head low, he reached the wooden post to which he had been tied while Clem had hurled those broad-bladed knives at him to try to make him talk. Now it afforded him a little cover against the flying lead.

The outlaws in the ranch were trapped. There was no way of escape for them and they knew it, but they elected to stay and fight with the courage and bitter savagery of cornered rats. Throwing two quick shots in the direction of the house, Bart rushed forward. Bullets skipped around his feet and unseen hands seemed to clutch at his sleeves and jacket as he pounded across the wide courtyard and flung himself the remaining five feet to come up hard against the solid brick of the walls. There was a window less than three yards away, but whoever lay behind it, although he had seen Bart's mad dash, could not fire upon him without exposing himself to the other's gun. Bart lay quiet for a moment, fighting to get air down into his heaving lungs. His heart was thumping madly against his ribs and there was a faint throbbing at the back of his eyes. Out of the edge of his vision, he saw that the troops were still moving in, firing as they came.

Nearby, from somewhere inside the house a man uttered a short, hoarse cry of pain and a moment later, the head and shoulders of one of the outlaws showed through one of the windows. The man hung there, arms hanging limply downward as though trying to reach for something on the ground, something that was just out of reach. Bart eyed him warily for a moment, then disregarded him. Pulling himself upright, and pressing his body close to the sun-warmed wall, he edged his way to one side, towards the window through which the man had fallen. There was just the possibility that this had been the only man in that room and if he could once get inside, it might be possible for him to find Zena Clayburne before the troops did. This woman was utterly evil, he told himself fiercely, and she had to die. There was always the chance that she might be able to wriggle out of any charge made against her, just as she had before when Sheriff Keene had died.

Cautiously, he moved to the window, risked a quick glance inside, peering over the dead outlaw's body. The room beyond was empty. Without hesitation, he climbed in and dropped to the floor, guns in his hands, ready to spit death. The men on the other side of the ranch were sweeping in now, gradually beating back the defenders. Bart tried the door, felt it open under his fingers. He was at the side of the house and there was a long corridor in front of him, with half a dozen doors opening off at intervals along it. Warily, he went forward, eyes flicking from side to side. One of the doors was open and as he approached, he heard a woman's voice raised in anger.

'Stay where you are, you coward,' Zena's voice. There was no mistaking the scorn in it. 'No one will ever drive me off my land. This is rightfully mine and I intend to fight to keep it.' A pause, then: 'Good Lord, man, don't you know how to handle a rifle?'

Bart edged forward and peered in through the open door. Zena Clayburne stood with her back to him, on one side of the far window. In front of her, cringed the black servant. He had a rifle in his hands, and he was shaking like a leaf. Not even the threat of his mistress could stop him from trying to

153

twist away from her grasp. A bullet smashed the glass in the window and the negro turned to run, his eyes wide with fear. Neither of them were aware of Bart's presence there. For a long moment, he stood watching the drama which was being enacted in front of him, sensing that something was about to happen, not sure why he felt like that. The negro tried to turn and run back into the middle of the room, then yelped in fear and pain as something flicked through the air like a striking snake. The lash whipped around his bare shoulders, biting deeply into the skin. Zena Clayburne's face was terrible to see. She lifted her right arm again, bringing the whip slashing down over the other's face as he went down on his knees in front of her, holding the heavy rifle loosely in his hands. Again and again, the whip landed on his shoulders as he knelt there.

'Get back to that window, damn you, and keep firing.' She hissed the words at him. As she raised her arm to strike him again, he lurched to his feet, stood for a moment swaying drunkenly in the centre of the room. Very slowly, he lifted the rifle and moved towards the window. Bart could see the other eyeing the whip which Zena still held in her hand, ready to use it again if he disobeyed her.

Apparently, he did not move fast enough for her. Her arm scarcely seemed to move, but the tip of the lash was across the other's shoulders once more. What happened next was so swift that there was no chance for Bart to move forward and intervene. Swinging abruptly, the negro lifted the rifle in his hands, but the long barrel was pointed not out of the window at the advancing troops, but directly at the woman. What was about to happen must have come to her in the split second before the other pressed the trigger. The sound of the shot was deafening to that small room. For an instant, she stood there, arms hanging loosely at her sides. The expression on her face seemed to change very slowly.

Shock and fear and terror were all blended in that look as she staggered back. The ugly red stain on the front of her dress began to widen ominously as she fell against the wall. The whip dropped from her grasp and fell clattering to the floor. She made one last effort to go forward, arms stretched out blindly in front of her, then her strength seemed to leave her and she collapsed forward at the negro's feet.

With an effort, Bart forced himself to move. Stunned by what he had just witnessed, he walked into the room, went up to the negro and took the gun from his unresisting fingers.

'She tried to whip me,' said the other dully. His lips scarcely moved as he spoke. 'I didn't want to get the gun to kill the soldiers. But she made me do it.'

Bart stood for a long moment, staring down at the woman who lay at his feet. Her face, frozen into a look of horror, held none of the beauty that he had first glimpsed when he had first met her. He was still standing there when the colonel came into the room.

'It's almost finished,' said the other tightly, then stopped. He came forward slowly, looked down.

'The negro killed her,' said Bart very quietly. 'She tried to make him fire on your men and when he refused, she used that whip on him. Poor devil. He looks as though he's been whipped before, not once, but many times. I'm surprised he didn't try to kill her before now.'

'From what I've heard about her, I'm surprised that somebody else hasn't done it,' remarked the other grimly. 'It's odd that a woman as beautiful as that should be so evil. She wanted everything that she saw, no matter what it was.'

'What do we do about him?' Bart nodded towards the negro, standing in the middle of the room.

'Nothing much we can do. I doubt if any jury in the country would convict him of murder. She's dead and we'll have no more trouble from her. As to what will eventually happen to the ranch and spread, that's up to the new sheriff of Cochita City once the people get around to electing one.'

'I reckon that if he's as good as Sheriff Keene, things will be all right,' said Bart' with a faint grin. 'I'm only sorry that I never meet him.'

The Colonel nodded, but said nothing. He went over to the door and gave orders to the sergeant who stood outside in the corridor. Then he came back into the room. 'We took a few of the men prisoners,' he said softly. 'They'll be taken back to the Fort and held there pending trial. I think they'll give us all the information we need.'

He went out of the room, then paused in the doorway. 'By the way, there's someone asking for you outside. It could he important.'

'I'll be right there,' said Bart quietly. He threw one last glance at the woman lying on the floor, then turned quickly on his heel and went out of the room which had seen so much violence. Outside, even though the air was hot and filled with dust, he drew a deep breath of it into his lungs and felt better for it. Slowly, he made his way into the courtyard, paused as a slim figure near the corral suddenly turned then came running towards him.

'So it's all finished, Bart,' Tess's eyes were shining as she came up to him. 'Now there's nothing to be afraid of any more. They can start rebuilding the town as it was before she came here.'

'Not as it was then,' Bart said slowly. 'This time, there'll be something new and big to build. Cochita City has a big future in front of it. Now that we have law and order again, the trail herds will start moving this way again and not all of them will go on to Abilene. We'll build stockyards here, get the railroad to run through from the east. The North is crying out for beef and we have all the cattle they need, and more, down here. All it needs is the means of getting them to where they're needed.'

'But first we'll need a sheriff who can make certain that no one like Zena Clayburne can bring death and terror to the territory again.' She came close to him, pressing her slim body against his. 'I had a talk with Ben Wheeler before I came

156

out with the soldiers. He told me about everything you did to help the townsfolk and how scarcely any of them backed you up. I think they're all ashamed of themselves now and they're looking for a way to thank you.'

'I don't need any thanks for what I did,' he told her. 'Besides, you're forgetting that I made a solemn promise that I'd hunt down those killers to the last one. Now that I've done it, I think I can sleep in peace.'

Tess looked at him solemnly for a moment, then said quietly. 'I think you ought to know that they elected their new sheriff a little while ago, Bart. The decision was unanimous.'

'Then I only hope they've chosen someone like Sheriff Keene,' he said fervently.

'I think they have – Sheriff,' said Tess softly. 'I don't think they could have chosen a better man.'

For a moment, Bart paused, taking in the full implications of what she had said, then he forced a grin. Together, they walked forward towards the waiting horses.